BOWLING BLUNDER

STELLA BIXBY

Sue,
I hope you
enjoy Bowling Blunder!

XOXO,
Stella
Bixby

FERRY TAIL PUBLISHING LLC

W e sounded like a herd of elephants running down the dirt road.

Elephants that giggled like schoolgirls.

"How is everyone doing?" I turned to jog backward so I could see the group. My headlamp shone against the dark of the early morning light. Five headlamps shone back at me.

"Do we have to go so far?" Amy croaked. Her dyed orange hair and baggy sweats made her look like a grandma wearing her teenage granddaughter's wardrobe.

"Oh, stop it," Fran said. "Ellie's trying to get us in shape for this run. Do you want to win the old people category or not?" Fran wore jeans like she did every day for every activity. Including yoga.

"Speak for yourself," Katie said, trotting along gracefully, her long blue wrap flowing behind her like a cape. "Some of us do not consider ourselves old."

Next to her ran another woman, equally as graceful, but in an outfit that looked like it came straight out of a

Los Angeles spin class. Bonnie was the odd one out, and it showed. None of the other women even acknowledged her existence.

I kept jogging backward. "You're not old. You're experienced."

"Ooh, experienced," Nancy, in her bright red tracksuit and matching tennis shoes, said as she power-walked near a panting Amy. "I like that."

"Don't be weird," Fran said. "She meant experienced in life. Not . . . other things."

Fran was the tough one in the group. She ran the feed and fabric store in the middle of Cliff Haven, Iowa—the town I'd recently come to know as home.

After being practically on my own for twenty-some years—transferring in and out of foster homes before settling into the solo life—I received a letter from my biological grandmother—Esme Vanderwick. Though I hadn't met Esme before she died, she did leave me her farm.

Now, Cliff Haven was more of a home than any I'd ever known.

Well, besides my Volkswagen Microbus—Mona.

Penelope, my tiny pet pig, and I lived many years in Mona. She had not only been my traveling wellness business—Relief with Ellie—she was my bedroom, bathroom, kitchen, dining room, and transportation. She was also relatively temperamental. It added to her charm.

"We're going to pick up the pace for thirty seconds," I said. "In five, four—"

"How fast do we have to go?" Amy whined, clutching her sides.

"Just as fast as you feel comfortable," I said. "In five, four, three—"

"I'm ready, just say go," Nancy said.

I laughed. That's what I was trying to do. "Five, four, three, two—"

"Hold on, my leg is cramping," Fran said, stopping to rub her calf.

"I'll circle back for you," I said. "Everyone else, thirty seconds, go."

All the women besides Fran took off. And when I say took off, I mean they seemed to go faster.

Maybe.

All but Katie and Bonnie were still practically walking. But Katie and Bonnie seemed to be in some sort of unofficial race. They might not have acknowledged one another, but they sure had a competitive nature.

Bonnie came to Cliff Haven under sketchy circumstances. She was having an affair with one of the local farmers who ended up dead in my cornfield. Through a series of events, Bonnie ended up getting his farm. Which was right next to mine. So when she'd shown interest in the morning running group, I couldn't turn her down. Plus, the extra money was always welcome.

"What's wrong with your leg?" I asked, running back to meet Fran.

"It's just a cramp," she said, still massaging.

"Can I help?"

"Sure," she said. "Give those magic fingers a whirl."

Whether my fingers were magic was still up for debate.

"I like what you've done with your hair," she said as I worked my way down her calf.

3

"It pretty much does whatever it wants anymore," I said.

My hair, unlike my fingers, was somewhat magical. At least in the sense that it changed color and shape whenever I had any sort of emotion. It also notified me of danger, but I was still working out the details on that one. The last time it had warned me, I hadn't paid attention and nearly got myself killed.

"I like the pink on you," she said. "It goes well with your eyes."

"I think pink means I'm happy," I said. "Especially when it's wavy like this."

I had it back in a ponytail, but the wave was still noticeable. "How's that feel?"

Fran flexed her foot. "Magical."

"Great," I said. "Now, let's catch up to the others."

"Race ya," she said and took off. She was almost as fast as Katie and Bonnie, but not nearly as fast as me. If I'd been able to stay at a high school for longer than a couple of months, I probably would have done well on a track team—maybe even gotten a college scholarship.

I passed her quickly and made my way up to the front of the pack.

"How are you feeling today?" I asked the two leaders, who each acted as if they were running solo.

"Feeling good," Bonnie said. "I like when it gets colder, and the air stings my lungs a bit."

I couldn't quite tell in the dark, but I think Katie may have rolled her eyes.

"I feel *great*," Katie said, trying to one-up Bonnie. "I

can't wait to knock the socks off everyone at the Trot 'n Tater this year."

"The what?" I laughed. Being from Colorado, I knew little about Iowa traditions.

"The Trot 'n Tater is the 5k we have every year the week of Thanksgiving," Katie said. "That's what those old ladies —" she shouted over her shoulder, "—were talking about."

"I get the trot part, but what's up with the tater?"

"Once the race is over, you have to eat a Tupperware full of mashed potatoes. If you throw up, you lose."

"What?" I laughed. "That's nuts."

"It's a very important tradition," Katie said but laughed along with me. "It takes stamina and an appetite."

"Sounds—uh—interesting." I checked my watch. "Okay, time to slow down and take a breather."

Everyone slowed to a walk, even Katie, but she waited until Bonnie did first.

"Did I hear you telling her about the TNT?" Amy yelled from behind us. "Can you eat, Ellie?"

Katie, Bonnie, and I slowed and waited for the others to catch up.

"Have you never seen her at a potluck?" Fran said. "She could be a professional eater."

"As long as the mashed potatoes don't have pork in them," Nancy said.

I laughed. She'd once tried to get me to eat a pork tenderloin, but I had to refuse. Not that I was a vegetarian or vegan. I just couldn't eat something that could be related to my best friend in the entire world.

"Let's place our bets now," Amy said. "Ellie's gonna win."

"I don't know," Nancy said. "Sometimes we get some good ones from the cities."

"But those ones don't know how to eat." Katie jogged practically in place to keep her heart rate up. "They're all a bunch of runners who barf everything up. I think we got ourselves a winner here."

Bonnie didn't join in the chatter. She never did. She kept to herself and barely even spoke to me.

I didn't know what to think about the Trot 'n Tater, but if there were two things I did relatively well, they were running and eating. And I wasn't about to tell them this, but mashed potatoes were one of my favorite side dishes ever.

I'd only ever had a real family Thanksgiving once with a foster family. I was five and Thanksgiving dinner ended with me going back into the system. One of the other foster kids intentionally spilled cranberries all over my brand-new white dress. Which naturally made my hair go all different shades of red and completely freaked out my foster parents.

All my other Thanksgivings were spent in either group homes or with families that didn't really celebrate.

"So? Will you race?" Nancy asked.

"What do I get if I win?" I asked.

"A big old trophy," Amy said. "In the shape of a potato with legs and wings."

I shook my head. I should have known it would be something like that.

"Should we do one more sprint before we call it a day?" I asked. "We're almost back to the house."

My house—the one I'd inherited from my grandmother—was at the end of a long dirt driveway that used to be surrounded by cornfields. Now that it had been harvested, it was just a big flat piece of land with a touch of snow that fell a couple of weeks back.

Northern Iowa wasn't like Colorado. Or at least Denver, Colorado. Once the snow came, it was there until spring. At least, that's what I'd been told.

"In five, four—"

But before I could get any further, a woman came running up behind us yelling obscenities.

We turned to look.

She wore all black with a bright reflective strip down each leg. When our headlamps caught the strip, it glowed like an agile worm dancing on its tail.

"I'm sorry, did we do something?" I asked as she ran by. She was still yelling.

When she realized I was talking to her, she held up a hand for me to be quiet and pointed at her ear.

I instantly understood—she was on the phone.

"You can't take me off the case," she went back to yelling. "I don't care what your reasoning is. She wants me on the case. And she is the client."

Once she was a few steps ahead of us, Fran said, "What in the heck was she talking about?"

"She was on the phone," I said. "Sounded important."

I shrugged. It wasn't our business. "Okay, let's do this one last sprint. In five, four—"

7

"I'm gonna win," Fran said, taking off before I got through my countdown.

Everyone else started running—even Nancy, who practically never ran.

"That's cheating," Nancy said, her sweet rosy cheeks bobbing up and down with every step. She and her husband were like the rock 'n roll equivalent of Santa and Mrs. Claus with their white hair, tattoos, and jolly nature.

It was too bad their son turned out to be a murderer. He killed his aunt, uncle, and cousin to get his hands on the family farm. In the end, it reverted back to his uncle's mistress—Bonnie—who was currently trying to get a permit to build a bunch of fancy houses on the land.

Those houses would go up right next door to mine. Thankfully, quite a few acres of my cornfield separated our properties.

The whole situation had shaken the community pretty badly. Nancy's son and his girlfriend had gone to jail because of it. Nancy and her husband, Hank, didn't like talking about it.

That was part of the reason I started the morning fitness club. Katie mentioned the other women needed a stress reliever. So every day, we worked out together, and then we each headed to our respective jobs. Mine being a waitress at the café.

Though I could probably get by on the money Esme left and the money I got from training sessions like the morning workouts with the ladies, I enjoyed working at the café a couple of days a week. It kept me connected in the community and gave me an outlet for my extroverted-ness.

I was just thankful I could use my degree in therapeutic recreation every once in a while if only to help my friends.

"I win," Katie shouted when she barely outpaced Bonnie and reached the top steps of my house. Penelope oinked excitedly and ran around Katie's feet. She loved it when we came back from runs.

I scooped her up and said goodbye to all the women. "I'll see you bright and early for yoga tomorrow."

"Namaste," Amy said with a bow, her orange hair flopping over her face.

Fran laughed. "You goof." Then she turned to Katie. "Next time, I'm going to win."

"Next time, don't cheat, and maybe I'll let you," Katie said.

"Oh, and Ellie," Fran said as I opened the door. "Start training that stomach of yours to eat after runs. We'll be counting on you next week."

I waved and waited until they were all out of the driveway before I went upstairs to shower.

2

W hen I first arrived in Cliff Haven, I felt guilty using Esme's space. But I'd tried to sleep in nearly all the other rooms, and none of them even remotely worked out for me. I always ended up sleeping in Mona.

Then I slept in Esme's bed. And it was as if Esme had made all the other beds intentionally unwelcoming so hers would feel so cozy it made it hard to get out of bed in the morning. Which was quite the task since I was one hundred percent a morning person.

The bedroom was the largest in the house, and in one corner down by the lower trim was a tiny hole just big enough for a finger to fit inside. That hole opened a secret passageway leading to an attic. I was almost entirely sure no one but Penelope and I knew about the attic.

And I planned on keeping it that way.

The attic was my sanctuary. The place I went when everything was too much, too overwhelming, too crazy. And I knew it was Esme's sanctuary, too. Her journal had told me that, if nothing else. I was still trying to figure the darn thing out.

The master bedroom, bathroom, and closet were almost four times as big as my living space inside Mona. Sometimes the expanse of the house actually made me claustrophobic. Or maybe the opposite—whatever that was.

I never liked super small spaces, but Mona's living area had always seemed perfect for Penelope and me. We would lie together and look up through the skylight at the stars every night.

As much as I loved Esme's—my—bed, sometimes I'd pull Mona out of the garage and sleep under the clear sky for old times' sake.

When I finished showering, I pulled on a pair of loose-fitting jeans and a nice long-sleeved t-shirt I'd gotten from Katie. She'd given me all of her daughter's old clothes. Her daughter—Melody—was a big-name actress and apparently had fancy Hollywood clothes now.

I'd never met Melody, but Katie was hopeful she'd come home for Thanksgiving this year. From what Earl—Katie's husband and Melody's dad—said, Melody hadn't been home in several years.

It was really none of my business, but people just seemed to like to tell me things. Personal things. Things I sometimes wished they wouldn't.

"I'll see you later," I said to Penelope. "Be good while I'm gone."

As I drove past Bonnie's house, I could see her in the large window watering her flowers.

I waved, and she waved back—her hands covered in yellow rubber gloves.

Bonnie seemed to be incredibly particular about everything. Her appearance, her home, her business. It didn't surprise me at all that she would do chores with gloves on.

When I pulled into town, the sky was lightening from a deep navy blue to a cool purple.

I unlocked the door to the diner and let two of the four regulars inside. I'd become familiar with two of the farmers—Hank and Earl. But these two—George and William—had kept their distance.

Probably because their wives thought I was a witch.

When I'd first arrived, everyone seemed to have loved Esme. They were always telling me how important she was to the town, how much they missed her, and how I reminded them of her.

But I'd come to realize not everyone loved Esme. And those people steered clear of me too. Including William and George, their wives, and their kids.

Jake—the local police chief and the man I once wrongly thought was my father—assured me they'd come around. Though wasn't sure, I wouldn't let it get me down. I'd learned early in life not to let the small things get to me. Or the big things. Or anything. I tried my absolute best to be happy regardless of my situation.

I set two cups of coffee in front of George and William and put their food orders in with the kitchen before tending to a woman who just walked in.

A woman I'd seen only once before.

"Can I get you something to drink?" I asked, handing her a menu.

"Don't you recognize me?" She wore more makeup than people usually wore in Cliff Haven and would have probably been prettier without it. She had on a button-down plaid shirt, a puffy green vest, skinny jeans, and brown lace-up boots. "I'm PJ's fiancée."

I almost corrected her because PJ was dead, but I didn't think it would be the kindest thing to do.

"That's right," I said. "I saw you at the hospital."

"I thought you were a cop," she said. "That man you were with was a cop, right?"

"He's the police chief."

"And you are?"

"I'm a waitress and recreational therapist," I said. "I was just helping Jake—the chief—with the investigation."

"And it was your boyfriend who killed him, right?"

"My boyfriend?" I was confused. Did she think I was Sally? "No, his girlfriend—Sally—is in jail as well. For helping him commit the crimes."

"Then who are you?" she asked.

Who was I? Her fiancé's ex-girlfriend, her ex-future-mother-in-law's neighbor. "I'm Ellie," I finally said. "And you are?"

"Samantha," she said. "Not Sam. Not Sammy. Samantha."

She dropped her head to look at the menu. "Coffee, black," she said without looking back up.

I didn't mind her rudeness. I couldn't imagine losing my fiancé, not that I'd ever been engaged, but still. And going through a court battle probably wasn't very fun.

When I dropped the coffee off, she ordered two egg whites and one slice of dry wheat toast.

"Who's that?" Bex said when she walked in to start her shift.

"That is PJ's fiancée, Samantha."

"Why is she here?" Bex was breathtakingly gorgeous with her black curly hair, dark complexion, and deep brown eyes. She almost always wore some version of the same outfit—bellbottom jeans, a flowy top, and sandals—even as the weather cooled.

"She said she's fighting Bonnie for the farm."

Bex huffed. "There has been enough fighting over that farm. It's bad luck if you ask me. There's too much bloodshed surrounding it."

The front door opened, jingle bells notifying us of Earl's arrival. Earl was Katie's husband and one of the more handsome of the older men in town with his salt and pepper hair and strong jawline. He was even more attractive when he smiled, which he didn't often do.

"I don't know that either of them actually wants to keep the farm," I said to Bex. "I think they want to develop the land."

"They might change their minds when they find out the town won't let that happen," Bex said.

"What do you mean?" I asked.

"She means," Earl interjected. "There's an ordinance in Cliff Haven that says no one can develop within city limits."

"But I thought we were outside city limits," I said.

"You are," he said. "But the very tip of Bonnie's property is in the city. She doesn't know that yet."

Bex gave me an amused smile.

"So basically, it's useless," I said. "And all those people died for something that would never come to pass, anyway?"

They both stopped smiling.

"When you put it like that," Bex gave me a sad face and walked away.

Earl patted me on the back twice, nearly knocking me over. "People die. It's sad, but it happens."

"It didn't have to happen," I said. "Ty didn't have to kill everyone."

"Ty was a greedy little boy who didn't want to lift a finger to make a buck." Earl's gruff mannerisms were intimidating at first, but the more I got to know him, the more he seemed like a big teddy bear.

"It's still sad," I said.

"You're right," he said. "It is sad. I may not have gotten along with Percy, but I never wanted him to die. And Helen was a good woman."

I nodded. I had really liked Helen, even though I hadn't known her very long.

A bell rang from the back, telling me I had an order ready.

I picked up Samantha's egg whites and toast and delivered them along with a coffee refill. "Can I get you anything else?"

"What did I hear you talking about?" Samantha said.

"When?"

"Just a minute ago," she said. "Did I hear that man say there's no way that land will be developed?"

I sucked in a breath. I didn't want to be the one to tell

her this. I hated confrontation. But I also couldn't lie. "Yes, that's what he said."

"And should I believe him?"

I shrugged. I didn't tell her he was a non-practicing attorney who had lived in Cliff Haven his entire life.

She pondered this for a second before looking back at me. "That's all."

Her dismissal was both rude and welcome. I didn't want to answer any more of her questions.

"Want to go out tonight?" Bex asked as we were cleaning and getting ready to close up. "A bunch of us are going into the city for some black light bowling and drinks."

I hesitated. I'd never been out with Bex and her friends before. They were the same age as me, but I felt much more comfortable around the older women.

"Come on, it'll be fun," she said.

"I don't know." I swept the entry near the door. Only a few people were left—one being Samantha, who had taken out her laptop and worked at her booth all day. She'd probably had fifteen cups of black coffee. If I had that much coffee, my hair would have worked itself into a giant fuzzball. "I have early morning yoga therapy tomorrow, and I probably shouldn't be hungover for that."

"You don't have to drink," Bex said. She'd asked me to hang out nearly a dozen times, and each time, I'd found a reason to decline. Not that I didn't enjoy hanging out with other people—that was one of my favorite things to do—I just knew some of her friends didn't like me.

"Okay, I'll go," I finally said.

Her eyes widened. "Really? That's awesome."

Anxiety crept up my spine, and I could feel my hair changing.

"Oh, come on, don't worry," she said, looking up at my hair. "My friends are nice."

I still found it disconcerting that many of the people in the town were not only unbothered by my hair changes, but also knew what they meant. Esme and Emily—my mother—had the same color-changing hair and had lived in Cliff Haven many years. But growing up, I'd always had to hide my hair. I had the scarfs, hats, and headbands to prove it.

"I guess I haven't had great luck with people my age," I said, taking a breath to get my hair back to its natural white.

"I'll be with you the entire time. Nothing bad will happen."

I felt a smidge better. "What should I wear?"

Before she could answer, a whirlwind of pink and sparkles entered the café. Four women screeched like banshees when they saw Samantha sitting in the corner.

Samantha closed her computer and jumped up to hug the short one with brown hair. Two of the other women were blonde, and one was . . . the woman who had been yelling into the phone on her run that morning.

She stood back from the group a bit but hugged Samantha tightly when it was her turn.

"Are you ready for the best bachelorette weekend ever?" The tall blonde asked, her peppiness that of a head cheerleader. "What do you have planned for us today?" she asked Samantha.

Samantha's eyes widened, then she turned her gaze on me. She told her friends to hold on and marched over with a big smile on her face. A smile she'd never given me before.

"Can I get you something?" I asked.

"As a matter of fact, you can," she said. "You teach exercise classes, right?"

"Therapeutic ones."

"What about pole dancing?"

I could feel my hair tingle with embarrassment.

Bex snickered behind me.

"Uh, no. That's not really in my wheelhouse." Or solar system.

"Maybe spinning?"

"I don't have spin bikes," I said. Or a proper studio for those bikes, but eventually I'd redo the barn and—

"Then what *do* you teach?" She huffed. "I want to do something for my friends. Something fun. I forgot today was up to me to plan. I'll make it well worth your while."

I thought for a minute. Part of me wanted to say no. Someone once told me it was my choice whether to make other people's emergencies my own. I could have easily told her no. It wasn't my fault she hadn't planned appropriately.

But it was hard to turn down the money. Though I had plenty to keep me going, I still had a fear of the bottom dropping out. I'd spent my entire adult life making sure I wouldn't go hungry—that Penelope wouldn't go hungry—I just didn't have it in me to turn down cold, hard cash.

"How about belly dancing?" I'd taught a class for a few months during my college internship. I wasn't great at it, but they didn't have to know that.

"Belly dancing?" Her eyes lit up. "Perfect. We'll be at your house in an hour."

I looked at my watch. I only had about thirty minutes left in my shift, which would only give me about twenty to prepare. "How about an hour and a half? I have to find some costumes."

"Costumes?" She smiled. "Perfect. Thanks."

3

I figured if anyone had costumes, Katie would. The minute my shift was over, I hopped into Mona and drove out of town toward Katie's farm.

"Hey there," Katie said when I knocked on the door. A rainbow of paint covered her face and bare arms.

"Is this a bad time?" I asked.

She looked down. "No." She laughed. "I'm painting a set for the Christmas play. I guess I got a little messy." She shrugged. "What can I do for you?"

"I wanted to see if you might have some type of costumes I might pass off as belly dancing skirts?"

She looked at me with wide eyes. "Are you taking up belly dancing, my dear?"

It was my turn to laugh. "I'm teaching a class this afternoon. A woman came into the café this morning and asked if I could. It never hurts to make extra money."

"Well, I don't think Melody has anything like that, but for a gala a couple of years back, we had a gypsy theme. I think I have some things left over from the photo booth if you want to look."

I sighed in relief. "Thank you so much."

She led me to her attic, where hundreds of totes lined the walls. Each was labeled with what it had inside and the event or play it came from.

"Here it is," she said, pulling one down labeled Gypsy Gala.

I carefully looked through the contents and came up with some gold chains that could easily wrap around the women's mid-sections and a few cute skirts.

"These are perfect," I said. "I promise I'll bring them back when I'm finished."

"I know you will," she said, walking me back downstairs. "Have fun in your class. If you need any tips, let me know." She shimmied her hips in perfect belly dancing fashion.

I laughed. It was no surprise she knew how to belly dance. Her daughter may have been the actress, but Katie could have easily graced the big screen.

I'd cleared out the formal dining room and made it into a makeshift studio for my early morning workouts with the ladies. Mirrors lined one wall, yoga mats stood in a corner, and a delicious diffuser that made the room smell like a whimsical spa sat on a shelf next to a picture of Penelope and me doing yoga at our favorite studio in Denver, Colorado, when she was just a piglet.

I laid out the costumes and checked the music to make

sure it was the belly dancing playlist I'd put together when I'd gotten back from Katie's.

Samantha and her crew showed up exactly an hour and a half from the time we'd spoken. Each of them wore black leggings and a bright pink t-shirt that said Janelle's Goddesses. I laughed to myself.

"Come on in," I said, opening the door. "We'll head into the studio."

"You look great," the tall blonde said. "Do we get to dress up too?"

I had on a long rose-colored crocheted skirt that tied at my hip with black leggings underneath and a cute tank top that I could easily pull up if I needed to show my mid-section.

"I have some costumes in here." I led them into the dining room studio, and their eyes widened at the sight of all the pretty colored skirts and belly chains.

Well, almost all their eyes widened. The short one with brown hair looked very uncomfortable. She held up a couple of skirts that might have been a bit too small and put them back before moving onto an overly large black and gold one.

She may have been a bit bigger than the other girls, but she didn't need to make herself look like a grandma. I should have never brought that skirt out.

I thought for a moment while the four other women put on tight-fitting skirts, belly chains and tied their t-shirts to show their midriffs.

"What about this one?" I asked, holding up one that looked perfect for her and was much more colorful.

"Do you think it'll fit?" she whispered. "I've lost some

weight for the wedding, but not nearly as much as I need to."

"I know it will fit," I said, handing it over. My scalp tingled in agreement. I was absolutely certain that skirt wasn't only going to fit, it would look perfect.

She slipped on the skirt and glanced in the mirror. It hugged her in all the right places.

"Wow," she said.

"Tie up your shirt, Janelle," the tall blonde said. "It's *belly* dancing. You have to show your belly." She smacked her own rock-hard abs that looked like they'd taken quite a lot of time and energy making. I worked out, but not enough to have a six-pack.

Janelle started to pull her shirt up, but I stopped her. "You don't have to. There are lots of belly dancers who don't pull up their shirts." I smiled. "You do whatever makes you comfortable."

The other women didn't seem as on board with it, but they smiled anyway.

"I mean, you are the bride," the short blonde said.

Samantha brought her friend—the bride who looked completely uncomfortable with the entire thing—belly dancing?

How mean.

At that moment, I made it my personal mission to make sure Janelle had a good time. The best time.

"Let's start with some stretches," I said.

We moved through motions to get them on the right track. I complimented Janelle most of all.

After a bit, I let them loose for a song. "I'll play something. I want you to feel the music. Don't overthink it. Feel your body, contract your abs, and have fun."

Instantly, Samantha took the spotlight. But the tall blonde—Missy—didn't seem to appreciate that, so she jumped in, and they started a belly dancing competition. It would have been humorous if they didn't look like they wanted to kill each other.

"How do you all know one another?" I asked Janelle.

"We went to college together," she said, moving her hips like a pro. "We were in the same sorority."

"That's great," I said. "What did you all go to college for?"

"I went for elementary education," Janelle said. I could totally see her as a kindergarten teacher. "Becky became a doctor." Becky—the short blonde—smiled.

Janelle continued, "Missy went for botany but ended up becoming an event planner."

"That's why I was the perfect choice for maid of honor," Missy said.

"If only you'd stop flirting with the groom," Samantha said, her tone irritated.

"Oh, it's no big deal," Janelle said to Samantha, then turned to me. "We've all flirted with each other's boyfriends or fiancés or spouses at one point or another."

"That is true," Becky said. "Remember that time Malen nearly decked Missy because she was flirting with that bartender?"

"That bartender was my high school sweetheart," Malen—the runner—said. She'd been the stiffest of all the women.

"If it makes you mad," I asked. "Why do you keep doing it?"

"Don't worry," Missy said. "Malen got me back. Remember that sailboat captain you practically stole right out from under me?"

Malen crossed her arms over her chest. "One, you cannot steal someone from someone else. People are not possessions. And two, he wanted to be with me." She blushed and looked at Samantha, who shrugged.

"No need to lawyer up on us," Missy said, raising her hands in the air. "It's all good. I was just saying."

"How about we talk about something else," Samantha said.

"Oh, Sammy, I'm sorry," Missy said in a sugary-sweet tone. "We're being super insensitive talking about our relationships when, you know . . ."

"It's perfectly okay," Samantha said. "And please, don't call me Sammy."

"Sorry," Missy said, but she didn't look sorry to me. "At least you'll get the farm out of it. As long as Malen does her job."

Samantha and Malen exchanged looks I couldn't decipher.

"I don't know if I want the farm anymore," Samantha said. "Turns out it can't be developed."

"What?" Janelle said. "But PJ said—"

"PJ was wrong," Samantha said. "And his mother will get a rude awakening when she finds out."

"So you're just giving up?" Becky asked.

"Not quite," Samantha looked at Malen and smiled. "We have a plan."

Oh boy. I did not need to hear this.

"Let's do one more song," I said. "And then we can move onto our cool down."

Everyone looked happy with that plan and dropped the conversation about the court case.

"What did you set up for tonight?" Janelle asked Samantha when we were lying on the floor in our final stretch.

"I thought we could go black light bowling." Samantha glanced over at me.

Was she really doing exactly what she'd heard Bex and I talking about?

"Bowling?" Missy said, sitting up. "Sounds boring."

"I think it sounds like fun," Janelle said.

Missy sighed. "I guess this is your weekend."

"Don't worry," Becky said. "Someday, we'll do this for you too. Whenever you decide to introduce us to Mr. Wonderful."

Missy giggled nervously. "Maybe."

"You're not making him up, right?" Janelle teased. "I mean, you won't even tell us his name."

"Maybe because I don't want you trying to steal him out from under me," Missy said.

Malen sighed. Samantha looked like she didn't believe a word Missy was saying.

"No one will steal your boyfriend," Janelle said. "I'm getting married, Samantha just lost her fiancé, Malen is happily married, and Becky is mostly happily married." She smiled at Becky. "But you better not accept a proposal before we get to meet him."

"When the time is right," Missy said. "I promise, you'll meet him. Name and all."

Janelle and Becky seemed appeased with this. Samantha and Malen acted like they couldn't care less.

"Well, ladies. That's time," I said. "I appreciate you coming to Relief with Ellie. It's been fun doing something I don't do very often." Or ever.

"What do you usually do?" Janelle asked.

"My actual business is more about recreational therapy —using recreational activities to help someone with physical, social, or emotional needs." I smiled. "It's been a passion of mine for a long time."

"I hear you're great at it," Samantha said. "The old farmer guys were talking about it this morning."

Ever since I'd helped one of them with his bad back, I had a reputation around town of being a healer. They thought it was magic. I assured them it was simply exercise.

"That's sweet of them," I said. "You can just put the costumes back on the table." They were all holding their skirts and chains. I'd have to wash them before I gave them back to Katie. A couple of the girls had worked up a decent sweat.

They each thanked me again, and on her way out the door, Samantha handed me five hundred dollars in cash. "Is that enough?"

Was she actually asking me that? "It's plenty," I said. "Too much."

"Dealing with the lot of them can be overwhelming," she said. "Plus, you made Janelle feel special after I dropped the ball. I'm just glad you and that other lady were talking about bowling today. I knew Janelle loved it, so it's the perfect way to make up for this blunder."

And in an instant, Samantha redeemed herself in my eyes. I still had so much to learn about not judging other people. "I guess I'll see you tonight."

She smiled. "Yes, you will."

"How do I look?" I spun around, showing Penelope the outfit I'd spent over an hour perfecting. I wanted to look cute but not overdone. I went with a pair of dark wash skinny jeans, sneakers, and a green t-shirt. I threw on a jacket for warmth and a scarf for protection. My hair had been a solid shade of pink since the belly dancing lesson, which would be great until it changed.

Penelope spun in a circle and oinked happily.

"Good," I said. "I like it too."

Bex would be picking me up in less than ten minutes, so I made sure all the lights were off, and Penelope was tucked in her little bed for the night. "I'm closing the piggy door," I said. "I'll be back late."

Penelope wiggled her snout at me, and I gave her a quick kiss on the head.

Bex drove a tiny car. It had enough room for five people, and she already had four. I scooched in the back next to one of Bex's friends.

"You guys know Ellie," Bex said. "She works with me at the diner."

Everyone said hi except the woman right next to me. She didn't look happy that I was sitting there. In fact, she had scooted so close to the woman on her other side, that woman had given her a funny look. I pushed myself all the way up against the door to give her more space.

"Next to you is Beth," Bex said. "She's lived in Cliff Haven her entire life and works at the library."

I'd never been to the town library. "It's nice to meet you, Beth."

Beth didn't look at me when she mumbled, "Nice to meet you too."

"You okay?" Bex asked Beth.

But Beth just nodded.

"Beth doesn't like witches," the woman on the other side of Beth said.

Ahh, so that was it.

"Ellie isn't a witch," Bex said. "She's a waitress."

"Then how do you explain her crazy hair?" the woman from the front said.

That crazy hair was about to get crazier. I could feel it sizzling at the roots.

"I think it must be a bad gene," I said with a laugh. Only Bex laughed with me. "But really," I said. "I'm not a witch. My hair isn't magical. None of me is."

It wasn't entirely true. I could sense things from time to time. But that wasn't magic like they were thinking. It wasn't like I could shoot sparks from my fingertips or make magic potions or anything like that.

"I heard your mother was magical," Beth said, her voice only loud enough to hear over the noise of the engine.

I turned in my seat to look at her. Hardly anyone wanted to talk about my mother. Jake had mentioned a few things, as had Sally before she'd gone to jail, but that was it.

"Who told you that?" I asked.

"My mom," Beth said. "She was a couple of grades ahead of your mom."

"And she said Emily was magical?" I asked.

"Don't sound so excited," Beth said, her voice no longer quiet. "It wasn't a good magical. She caused a lot of problems at Cliff Haven High. If she was a witch, she was a bad witch."

I could feel all the eyes in the car on me. "Does your mom know where Emily might be now?"

"No one does," Beth said. "She was trouble just like Esme was trouble just like yo—"

"How about we listen to some music," Bex said, cutting her off.

She turned the music up so loud it would obliterate any possible conversation. After a few minutes, I could feel my hair returning to normal, which meant the pretty pink sheen was probably white again. Not that the white was bad, it just wasn't as fun.

I pushed my shoulders back and looked out the window. I would have fun tonight, regardless of how Bex's friends felt about me.

4

"I am so sorry," Bex said when we all got out of the truck at the bowling alley.

"Don't worry about it," I said. "I've gotten worse over the years."

"I didn't know Beth felt that way. I would never have set you up like that. I feel terrible."

The other women walked ahead of us, occasionally glancing back. They were probably talking about me, but I didn't care. It's not like they were my friends.

"Really," I said. "It's okay. I'm perfectly fine. I came to hang out with you, not your friends."

Bex wrapped an arm around my shoulders. "You look gorgeous, by the way."

All the other women wore jeans and a sweatshirt or t-shirt, so I fit right in.

When we walked into the bowling alley, it took a minute to get my brain around everything that was going on. Black lights illuminated anything that was white—shoelaces, t-shirts, socks.

A small arcade with pinball and driving games occupied one side of the building. On another was the bar.

"You're bowling, right?" Bex asked.

I nodded and pulled out enough money to pay for my shoe rental and a couple of games.

"You'll be on lane twelve." The lady helping us pointed to the other end of the building. "The ones next to you have league teams, so don't get in their way."

We moved toward the arcade side of the building.

"Oh my goodness," Bex said. "Look who's here."

She pointed to the lane marked with a big number ten. Standing in a group huddle were Nancy, Katie, Fran, Amy, and a couple of women I didn't recognize. Further down—in the lane right next to the one we'd been assigned—was Samantha's group.

While Katie's group should have been dressed as a team—it being a league and all—each person wore styles befitting their personalities. On the other hand, Samantha's group dressed like a team, and they weren't even part of the leagues. They wore matching white t-shirts that said Bowl Me Over in a swirly pink glitter font and glowed under the black lights. On top of their heads were velvet headbands, and clutched in their hands were personalized water bottles. I wasn't quite certain how Missy had pulled off the shirts in such a short amount of time, but I had to admit they were pretty cute.

"Is that my mom?" Beth asked, pulling me out of my thoughts. "We cannot be right next to my mother."

Beth's mother must have been one of the women I didn't recognize in Katie's group.

Bex shrugged. "How was I supposed to know they had a bowling league up here?"

"Because it's the closest bowling alley to Cliff Haven," Beth said.

"She's *your* mom." Bex laughed. "Maybe you should keep better tabs on her."

Beth looked distraught. She probably didn't want to be seen with me.

"It'll be okay," I said. "We can still have fun. I'm sure they won't even notice us. They look pretty into their game."

Beth glared at me.

And ultimately, I was wrong. But it wasn't Beth's mom who saw us first. It was Nancy.

"Ellie, is that you?" She wore a red bowling shirt and sparkly red bowling shoes. "Look, ladies, Ellie's here."

Beth wasn't the only one in our group to glare at me this time.

The only one who didn't seem perturbed was Bex.

I waved at Nancy and the others.

"Come over here, I need you for good luck," Katie said, cradling a bowling ball in her arms like a baby.

I obliged. "I'll be right there," I said to Bex.

"We'll put you on the board," she said and walked away with her friends. Part of me just wanted to stay with the older ladies.

Except the two women I hadn't met were giving me looks similar to what Beth had been. Now that I looked closer, one was obviously Beth's mom. They had the same mousy brown hair, large eyes, and pursed mouth.

Katie held out her ball for me. "Give it some luck, would you?"

I reached out a hand, and Beth's mom gasped. She probably thought I was using magic.

"This is silly," I said, then placed my hand on the ball. "I'm sure you don't need any luck."

"Ooh, I can just feel it," Katie said. "I'm going to get a strike this time."

"You'll get a strike because you're the best one on our team," Beth's mom said. "Not because you need a witch's help."

Nancy, Amy, and Fran gasped.

Katie, who was lined up and ready to go, turned and walked back to the group.

I wanted to melt into the floor.

Both Bex's and Samantha's groups turned to watch.

"Belinda May, you will not start that witch business with our Ellie," Katie said, her voice calm yet firm. "I know you didn't get along with Emily, but that's ancient history."

Belinda looked like she might say something else, but the other woman I didn't recognize put a hand on her arm as if to stop her.

"Now," Katie said, a tone of finality in her voice. "I need to get this strike."

She winked at me before throwing the perfect strike right down the middle. It was almost as if the pins fell before the ball even touched them.

Katie turned and did a little curtsy.

"Thanks for the luck," she said when she got back to me.

"That was all you," I said, knowing full well I had nothing to do with her success. If anything, I would have had to rub my hair on her ball. And even if I thought that might do anything—which I didn't—I wouldn't do that. "I should probably head over and join my group."

"Good luck," Katie said. "Not that you'll need it." She winked, and I could see Belinda's face crumple in anger. Katie was not helping the fact people thought I was a witch.

"Ellie," Samantha said when I passed by her team.

"Oh hey," I said, acting as if I hadn't seen her. The other women in her group were gawking at me.

"What was that lady going on about, you being a witch?" she whispered.

"It's just a superstition about my family," I lied. "It's nothing to worry about."

"Okay," she said. "But I just want you to know—magic or not—our team is totally going to beat yours."

If only I weren't so competitive. "I guess we'll have to see."

She smirked, and I returned the glance before we both started laughing.

"But seriously," I said. "You're going down."

Bex handed me a bright pink sparkly ball once I'd laced up my shoes. "Have you ever bowled before?"

"Once in college." I shrugged. "But we have to beat them."

"Isn't that the woman from this morning?"

"I gave them a belly dancing lesson this afternoon," I said. "It was pretty fun."

"Belly dancing?" Bex laughed. "You are full of

surprises, Ellie Vanderwick. Okay, now just roll the ball down the center of the lane and knock down the pins."

I laughed at how simple she made it sound. "Aye aye, captain."

The other women in our group had cocktails in their hands and gossiped about people in town I'd never heard of.

I pulled the back of my shirt down, swung my arm back, and rolled the ball neatly toward the pins.

Just like Katie's had, my ball plowed them all over.

"Wow," Bex said. "You're a natural."

"Beginner's luck?" I shrugged.

"Or magic," Beth murmured under her breath.

I didn't justify her with a response.

"My turn," Missy called out, taking a sip from her water bottle before picking up her ball. "Don't forget to stay hydrated," she said to the others, who each dutifully took sips of theirs too. "We can't have hangovers ruining our week."

She hit three pins, and her shoulders slumped. "Maybe I need a bit of magic," she said to me.

I laughed. "There's no magic."

"I like magic," a man said, setting down a tray of drinks before coming up behind Malen and squeezing her middle. She quickly brushed him off.

"Chad," Samantha said. "What are you doing here?" She didn't look happy to see him either.

But the other three women smiled.

"I'm here to visit my wife and help with the case," he said, wrapping an arm around Malen's shoulders and handing her a drink from the tray. "I brought you your favorite."

"I can't believe you'd come here," she threw the drink in his face and walked away. So much for being happily married.

Samantha started to go after her, but Chad grabbed her arm. "Can I talk to you for a minute?"

If looks could kill, he'd be dead. But she followed him anyway to a small table where he used the paper napkins to clean himself up.

"Why is he busting in on your bachelorette party?" Becky asked Janelle.

Missy looked over at Samantha. "From what I've heard, he's taking over the case. Malen is not happy about it."

"Chad is taking over Samantha's case?" Janelle said. "Why?"

"I couldn't figure that part out." Missy shrugged. "I just heard Malen through the wall this morning. She sounded mad, then I think she threw her phone against the wall."

Apparently, Malen yelled on the phone a lot. I thought back to when she was running and yelling at the same time.

"Ellie, it's your turn," Bex said. "Let's see if you can make another strike."

I did.

And every ball after that resulted in a strike, too. I was starting to wonder whether I *was* somehow using magic. My hair may have changed on its own, but I'd never had something like this happen.

"Maybe more than beginner's luck?" Bex asked with a smile. "I guess I'm just glad I'm on your team."

Beth looked like she might lunge at me at any moment. She didn't seem thrilled about having me on her team.

Malen still hadn't come back, but Chad and Samantha had. Chad took over in Malen's place. Which I would guess Malen wouldn't love.

By the time the game was in the final frame, it seemed like the entire bowling alley was watching me. Katie, Fran, Amy, and Nancy cheered loudly behind us before the entire alley hushed.

With breath held, I released the last ball down the polished wood surface. My competitive nature came out even when I knew I should have thrown the game. Should have aimed for the gutter. If only to protect the fact that perhaps there might be more to this win than simple beginner's luck.

But this—like every one before it—perfectly hit its mark, toppling all the pins.

The crowd erupted as I stared unbelievingly down the alley. The machine dropped the arm to clean up the wreckage.

"Wow, that was amazing," Janelle said. "Tell me the truth." She leaned in closer to me. "Did you use magic?"

"No," I said once more. And I didn't think I had. My hair was behaving itself. There were no tingles. Nothing. If I had magic, wouldn't I feel it?

Several men offered to buy our group rounds of drinks, which Bex's friends happily allowed. Some of them even bought drinks for Samantha's group. None of them seemed overly worried that Malen had vanished.

Chad—Malen's husband—was actively flirting with Missy, tucking her hair behind her ear and casually grabbing her hand. Missy didn't seem to mind the attention. I didn't understand the dynamic of their group. Still, I didn't have time to contemplate it because at that moment, Nancy—practically hopping with excitement—rushed over with the other women to congratulate me.

"Did you see who's here?" Katie asked when she hugged me.

I followed her line of sight to find Bonnie standing in a corner next to the big rig game with Malen. They didn't seem to be in a very happy conversation.

By the way Bonnie was dressed—skinny jeans, a flowy white top, and a leather jacket—I suspected she wasn't here to bowl.

"How does she always make me feel frumpy?" Katie looked down at her own outfit then back over at Bonnie.

Katie wore a pair of salmon-colored gaucho pants and a white t-shirt tucked in with a long black cardigan wrap over top. The red and blue bowling shoes did little for the outfit, but Katie looked anything but frumpy.

"You look beautiful," I said. "You have your own style, which makes you stand out from the crowd. In a good way, of course."

Katie blushed. "You're too kind."

She led me back over to the group, which was still celebrating. All the older ladies had glasses of wine while Bex's friends and a growing group of men had beer. When I approached, they let out another cheer.

I hinged at the waist for a small bow, and the lights went out.

Complete darkness fell like a blanket covering the sun.

At first everyone was silent. Then a scream came from where Bonnie and Malen had been standing.

Chaos ensued, screams coming from all over the place.

My heart rate sped, and my scalp started to burn. Which usually meant danger.

I fumbled to find my phone in my satchel. There was a flashlight app on it that would help me locate Katie, Nancy, and the others to make sure they were okay.

Where was that stupid phone?

Someone bumped into me as they tried to figure out where they were.

My fingers finally came to rest on the phone, and I yanked it out. When I turned on the screen, the lights flickered back on.

People froze in their tracks. I glanced to where Bonnie and Malen had been standing.

Malen lay in a contorted position on the floor next to the arcade game.

And Bonnie was gone.

5

"Oh, for the love of Pete," Fran said. "Is that what I think it is?"

Amy glanced to where Fran was pointing and looked like she might faint.

"Come on, let's get out of here," Bex said.

But my feet were glued to the ground. It was like I couldn't go anywhere unless I went toward the body.

"What are you doing?" Katie asked. "You can't go over there."

But my feet had decided. I was, in fact, going over there.

My stomach turned when I saw Malen lying with her arms trapped under her and her face smooshed into the floor. It was like she had been doing downward dog and her arms collapsed. I reached down to find a pulse, but there was nothing.

Bonnie had been having a serious conversation with Malen, the lights went out, and then Malen—the lawyer fighting to take Bonnie's land—was dead.

It was almost too convenient.

Samantha and Janelle walked out of the bathroom, giggling about the power outage. When they noticed no one else was talking, they stopped to look around.

As Samantha's gaze fell on Malen's lifeless body, she let out a scream worthy of a horror movie.

She rushed over, flipped Malen over, and threw herself on top. "No," she yelled. "No, no, no. You're okay. Come on. Wake up." She shook Malen. "Malen. Malen!" She started doing some semblance of CPR. "Come on, Malen. Wake up. You can't die." Tears streamed down her face as Janelle looked on. Janelle was crying too but didn't seem as worked up as Samantha.

I glanced around to find Chad, but he seemed to have vanished.

"Samantha," I said, touching her shoulder.

She threw her arm back, hitting me straight across the face, then went back to pounding on her friend's chest.

I rubbed my cheek and said, "Let me do it. I know CPR." I also knew it probably wouldn't do anything other than make Samantha feel like I'd tried to do something.

Janelle came to pull her away. "Come on, let her help."

I got down on my knees and checked to see if Malen was breathing or had a pulse. It was no surprise that she didn't. I started CPR. As I did compressions, I noticed a syringe and a bunch of dust bunnies under the big rig machine. I looked up and down Malen's body. There were no noticeable marks where a needle might have stuck her. Though, the stick mark could have been under her clothes.

Her pretty sparkly t-shirt covered my hands in glitter,

and her headband bobbed every time I pushed on her chest.

The police arrived much faster than they would have in Cliff Haven. Jake—the Cliff Haven Police Chief—did his best, but when the police force was so small, they couldn't possibly cover ground like these big-city cops.

The paramedics came in next, assessed the situation, and hooked her up to an AED machine. They told me to stop compressions so the AED could determine whether to shock. But there was no heart rhythm. She was dead.

When a paramedic said as much, Samantha fell to her knees and dropped her head to the ground.

I knew I should have felt bad for Samantha—and I did —but another emotion was stronger. Jealousy. My hair was frizzing and probably turning an ugly shade of puke green.

I hated jealousy. All it did was make me want things I might never have. Like friends who would weep like that when I died.

I mean, Katie and Nancy would probably be pretty sad. Bex too. But I wasn't close enough to anyone for them to have that kind of reaction.

"Let's go home," Bex said, grabbing me by the arm.

"Not so fast," one of the officers said. "We need to speak with everyone before they leave."

I glanced around. The two people they needed to talk to weren't even there. Both Bonnie and Chad had disappeared.

Maybe there was no need to be suspicious. Maybe she had a heart attack or something. But my hair follicles felt singed from all the heat they were producing.

An officer stepped in front of me, blocking my view of Malen's body. "Why don't you wait over there, and we'll talk to you when we're ready."

He didn't have to be so pushy.

But I got it.

He had a crime scene to protect.

He didn't know I'd helped solve a crime only a few weeks before.

"Can you believe they're making us stay here all night?" Fran asked when I rejoined the group.

"Just until they can talk to us," I said. "It probably won't take all night."

"That's good because I need my sleep before you twist us into pretzels tomorrow morning," Amy said. "I'm sore enough from the run today."

I laughed. They were always complaining about how tough I was on them, but in reality, they'd all gotten stronger and more agile.

"I guess the good news is, if we're stuck here all night, we could just do our yoga under the black lights," I said.

"I'd like to see you do yoga in those tight jeans," Fran teased.

"So would I," a man said from behind me.

I turned to find one of the men who had insisted on buying us all a round of drinks when I won the bowling game. Winning the game seemed like ages ago now.

"I noticed you haven't had anything to drink," he said. "Can I get you anything? A water maybe?"

The power of suggestion turned my mouth into a desert. "Water sounds great."

He nodded and headed to the bar. Actually, behind the bar. Like he owned the place. Maybe he did.

"Dang, girl," Bex said. "That is one fine-looking man."

I smiled and glanced over my shoulder at him. He was tall and athletic, with dark skin and even darker hair.

"Beth's been trying to catch his eye all night, but he just keeps looking at you."

I laughed. "Beth can have him," I said. "As soon as he figures out about my—" I pointed at my hair. "—he won't want to be around me anymore."

"Someday, you'll have to trust that someone will accept you, crazy hair and all." Bex smiled.

Little did she know, I'd tried going that route. Even as recently as just before I'd gotten the letter telling me about Esme's farm.

"Here's your water," Mr. Hottie said.

"Thank you," I said. "I didn't catch your name."

"It's James," he said. "And you are?"

"Ellie," I said. "It's a pleasure to meet you."

"Where are you from, Ellie?" James took a sip of his water.

"I just moved to Cliff Haven from Denver, Colorado."

"Why?" He laughed. "I mean, don't get me wrong, I've lived in Iowa my entire life. But not many people move from Colorado to Iowa. It's usually the other way around."

"My grandmother left me her farm."

"So you're a farming yogi?" His smile was gorgeous. Everything about him was gorgeous. And yet, in the back of my mind, I knew it wouldn't work out. He was normal.

45

Probably just out of college looking for a normal woman to date. To love. To marry.

The thought made me both hopeful and terrified.

"I should probably get back to my friends," I said. "Thank you for the water."

He looked disappointed. "Wait," he said before I could get too far away. "Can we exchange numbers?"

I didn't know what harm that would do.

We handed each other our phones and typed in our contact information.

"There," he said. "If you ever want to hang out, let me know."

I put my phone back into my satchel and smiled. "I'll do that."

He watched as I turned. I could feel his gaze on me as I walked away.

"So?" Bex asked as Beth gave me the evil eye.

"His name is James. He gave me his number." I couldn't help but smile. I was a sucker for love. Or maybe for flirting. Either way, it always felt nice to be wanted.

"Ma'am, can we please speak to you?" A different officer tapped me on the shoulder. He was probably in his mid-fifties, had bright red hair and a tired smile.

I turned and nodded. "Sure."

"And then when we're done with her, we'd like to speak with the rest of you," he said to the group. "If you'd all like to follow me this way, we'll get you out as soon as we can."

Both Bex's and Katie's groups followed as the officer led me to a tiny back office that smelled like an over-worked and under-dusted computer and chewing tobacco.

I hadn't seen any of the girls from Samantha's group. They'd probably been spoken to first since they knew Malen.

"My name is Trent," he said when we sat down. "Can you please tell me your name and date of birth?"

I did.

"Great. Now, will you give me an overview of your evening?" He pulled a pad of paper and pen from his shirt pocket and waited for my response.

I told him about the game and how I'd won. Everyone was excited and cheering, and then the lights went out.

"And before the lights went out, did you see anyone in that general direction?"

I knew this was the moment I had to throw Bonnie under the bus, and I hated it. All signs pointed to her. But what if she didn't do it? What if it was a fluke? Maybe it was Chad.

"I think I saw a few teenagers playing the arcade games." I hesitated.

"Anyone else?"

"Malen—the victim—was talking with a woman named Bonnie." I felt horrible. I'd already falsely accused her of murder once. I didn't want to do it again. "She's my neighbor."

"Malen or Bonnie?"

"Bonnie."

"Where do you live?"

"In Cliff Haven." I gave him the exact address.

"I have some family up in Cliff Haven," he said. "My cousin is the police chief."

"Jake?"

He nodded. "I used to visit him every summer."

"He's a great guy," I said. "He and my mom dated in high school. And I helped him solve a case a few weeks ago."

"Ellie," he said as it looked like a lightbulb flashed on in his head. "Emily's daughter."

I smiled.

"I should have known. You look just like her." He glanced up at my hair. "She was a wonderful girl. I only wish she hadn't left. You know, I think that's part of the reason Jake became a police officer in the first place."

"Oh, yeah?" That didn't make much sense. "Why?"

"I think he thought being a police officer would somehow give him access to information normal people didn't have. That he'd be able to find her more easily."

If only he could. No one knew if she was even still alive.

"He told me about the case, triple homicide?"

I nodded. "It was pretty sad."

"I think it's great you helped him on his case, but we can handle our cases ourselves here."

"I'm sure Jake could have handled the case without me," I said.

"Do you have the gift like Esme? Is that why he let you help?"

I shook my head. "I don't have the feelings."

He looked confused. "Then why—never mind." He waved a hand in the air. "Let's just get back to the interview. I have a bunch more people to interview."

I sat up straighter in the chair. "Where were we?"

48

"You were talking about Bonnie and Malen and how they were talking just before the lights went out."

"Yes," I said. "They were. Talking."

"Did it seem like a friendly conversation?"

"It seemed tense," I said. "I'm not trying to say Bonnie did this because I don't think she did. But Malen *was* representing a case against Bonnie."

"Is that so?" He took down a note. "Do you know what the case is about?"

"It's between Samantha and Bonnie," I said. "Bonnie got the property when all those people died. But Samantha was Bonnie's son's fiancé, so she feels like she deserves the property."

"Funny, she didn't mention any of that," he said.

"Well, she probably didn't know Malen and Bonnie were talking. She was in the bathroom with the bride when it happened. I saw her and Janelle—the bride—walk out right after the lights came back on. They were laughing and joking, and then they saw Malen and Samantha lost it."

"So when the lights came back on," Trent said. "Did you see Bonnie leaving?"

"I didn't see Bonnie at all," I said. "But I did see a needle and syringe under the big rig game when I was giving Malen CPR."

He wrote that down. "We'll look for that. Thanks."

I wanted to point out that I'd just helped him but thought it was probably a bad idea. Plus, they may have already found the syringe.

"Did you notice anything else?" he asked.

"Malen's husband was here tonight too. She wasn't

happy to see him. When he handed her a drink, she threw it in his face and stormed away. Apparently, they're getting ready to divorce."

This perked him up a bit. "Do you know his name?"

"Malen's friends called him Chad."

"Did you see Chad and Malen together again before the lights went out?"

I shook my head. "And when the lights came back on, I didn't see him anywhere."

Trent nodded. "Thank you, Miss Vanderwick. You've been very helpful."

"Happy to help," I said with a smile.

"That's good, but we won't be needing any more help unless you remember something specific you saw or heard." He pulled out a business card. "If you do, let me know."

6

I nearly fell asleep in the car on the way home, but I didn't want to touch Beth and test my luck. One dead body was enough for one night. I didn't want to be the second.

Once I was clear of Beth, I fell into bed harder than a boulder on a highway.

My doorbell rang an hour before the yoga session was supposed to begin. Surely, it wasn't Katie and the gang.

I pulled myself out of bed and slipped my feet into the fuzzy slippers that kept them from coming into contact with the cold hardwood and brick floors.

The doorbell rang again before I could get to the door.

"I'm coming," I said as cheerfully as possible. I was a morning person, but this early was pushing it.

I flipped on the porch light and peeked through the curtain on the window next to the door. Standing in the dim porch light shivering was a very distressed-looking Bonnie. Her white blouse was rumpled and torn, and her salt and pepper hair was sticking up at all different angles.

She pounded on the door again. "Ellie?"

I opened the door, and she walked into my house, pushing past me. "Something happened."

"I can see that," I said, closing the door. "Are you okay?"

"Okay?" Bonnie asked. "I am most certainly not okay."

Penelope oinked from the top of the stairs. I'd left her in the bedroom upstairs, thinking she'd stay asleep and she wasn't good at going down stairs.

I walked up and brought her back down. "Let's go in the living room."

She followed me in and sat perched on one of the armchairs.

"Can I get you anything to drink?" I asked.

"Do I look like I need a drink?" Bonnie glanced at the door. "Don't answer that." She shook her head. "You were at the bowling alley, right?"

I nodded.

"That's what I thought, but my mind is all fuzzy," she said.

"What do you remember?" I asked.

If she killed Malen, she might have been putting on an act. I had to be careful what questions I asked, but I also didn't want to accuse her of murder. Again. I'd done that once before, and it's one of those moments you replay in your head when you're trying to go to sleep—the ones you analyze repeatedly, wishing you could have done something differently.

"I went to the bowling alley to see if I could join in Katie's game." She looked down at her hands. "She said no. Not that

I expected a different answer, but I hoped." Her shoulders lifted into a shrug. "And then, the lights went out, and the next thing I knew, I was in my car freezing my butt off."

"Do you remember talking to Malen?" I asked.

"The attorney?" Bonnie rubbed her upper arm. "I think. Maybe."

Either she was a phenomenal actress, or she was genuinely having a hard time remembering.

"Do you remember what you were talking about?"

"I'm sure it was about the land." Her eyes lit up. "She was telling me I couldn't legally develop the property. I think she was about to offer me a settlement when the lights went out."

"And then what?" I asked. "The lights went out and . . ."

She dropped her head into her hands. "I'm sorry. That's all I remember."

I stayed silent, waiting for her to tell me more.

"Do you think Malen did it? Drugged me and took me to my car?"

I shook my head no.

"How can you be so sure?"

"Because Malen's dead," I said, trying to pick up on any bit of a reaction she might have.

Her fingers, interlaced in her lap, paled as if she were squeezing her hands together. "What do you mean, she's dead?" Her words were even but nervous.

"When the lights came back on," I said. "You were gone, and she was on the ground dead."

Her jaw dropped open. "Oh no," she said. "This can't

be happening." She stood and started pacing the room. "They'll think I did it. It looks like I did it, right?"

I nodded.

"Do you think I did it?" she asked.

I searched my scalp for feelings, but there were none. "No," I said. "I don't."

"Then you can help me." Her eyes glazed with tears. "You can help prove I didn't do it. You solved PJ's case. You can solve this one too."

"I don't think it'll be that easy," I said, remembering Trent's dismissal of my help. "This isn't Jake's case. And even if it was, I'm not a cop. I can't just go around investigating random cases."

"Come on. Everyone knows you're a witch. That's how you caught Ty," she said. "This would be easy for you."

I sighed. It was too early for this.

Penelope gave me a warning oink, alerting me that my hair was changing color. Thankfully, Bonnie had seen my hair change. Which was probably why she'd jumped on board the witch train.

"I'm not a witch," I said. "I didn't catch Ty using magic. I caught him by being observant."

"Then be observant," Bonnie said, waving a hand around. "I don't care how you did it. Just help me figure this mess out. And quick."

I glanced at the clock next to Bonnie on the fireplace mantel. The other women would be arriving shortly.

I took a breath. "If you agree to go to the police station and report what happened to you, I'll look into it."

She hesitated before saying, "Don't you think they'll

simply arrest me and be done with it if I waltz right in there?"

"If you did nothing wrong," I said. "Then you are simply going there to report a crime against you. They can't arrest you unless they have good reason."

"Fine." She sighed. "I'll go to the police station. But you have to look into it."

"I will." I didn't tell her how far I'd go looking into it, which would probably not be very far. "Now, how about I make us some coffee before the others get here? We both know Katie will be itching for her caffeine."

Bonnie wrinkled her nose at the mention of Katie.

"I don't understand why you don't like Katie." We walked to the kitchen with Penelope tight on my heels.

"She hates me because Percy and I had an affair."

"I'm not sure that's why she dislikes you." I didn't think Katie cared much about what Percy did. It wasn't like she and Helen—Percy's wife—had been good friends. And now that Percy and Helen were both deceased, Bonnie was pretty inconsequential to Katie's life. Well, besides the fact that Bonnie was planning on ruining Katie's view.

Bonnie sat on a bar stool at the island in my kitchen. "It's because of the development, isn't it?"

I nodded.

"But it would do so much good for the town."

I thought about that a minute. "Like bring in more people?"

"Residents *and* visitors."

"Visitors?" Because I'd lived in Colorado, I was well versed in the importance of tourists. Iowa didn't get many of those. At least not as many as Colorado had. "How would you do that?"

"Didn't you hear?" she asked.

"Hear what?"

"I'm planning on building a massive event and recreation center in addition to the housing." She sipped the coffee again. "People who buy homes like I build expect to have recreation at their disposals and more than just a traveling therapeutic recreation van. No offense."

"None taken." She had a point. "But why would these people move to Cliff Haven?" I asked. "Not that there's anything wrong with Cliff Haven," I added quickly. "But why?"

"It's beautiful and quiet here," she said. "Especially when you venture into the state parks."

"What will they do for work?" It wasn't like everyone could work at the café or the hardware store.

The thought of the hardware store touched on a nerve. Helen's Hardware was being torn down and replaced by a chain hardware store. By the woman sitting in front of me.

"We don't need to talk about it," Bonnie said, glancing up at my hair.

I pulled a piece out from behind my ear to find the natural white streaked with red. "Sorry," I said. "I was just thinking of the hardware store."

Bonnie didn't respond.

A knock at the door interrupted the awkward silence.

"Oh good, the ladies are here," I said.

"I need to run home and change before class." Bonnie

stood. "Can I go out the back? I don't want them to see me like this."

I wasn't sure I wanted to let her out of my sight. What if she ran? But the knocking continued, more adamant now. "Okay, I'll see you in a few minutes, right?"

"Don't worry. I won't take off."

When I got to the door, it wasn't Katie, Amy, Fran, or Nancy.

It was Samantha.

I pulled open the door.

Samantha's eyes were puffy, her face splotchy, and her hair—still in the velvet headband—messy.

"I need your help." She tried to push past me, but I held my ground this time. I was tired of people barging into my house.

"I'm sorry your friend died," I said. "But I don't know how I can help."

"Someone killed her, and I think they're after me too," Samantha said. "I just need your help to prove it."

"I can't prove anything. I'm not a—"

"Witch? Yeah, I know. Witches aren't real."

"I was going to say cop. I'm not a cop." I sighed. "But I'm not a witch either."

"But you figured out that Ty was the bad guy last time. You. Not the police."

"They would have figured it out. They probably already had." I didn't want to discredit Jake. He was a fantastic police officer. And, from what I could tell, Cliff Haven PD was very well-versed in these things.

"I don't care about how capable you think the police

are," she said, obviously getting frustrated. "They weren't able to stop Ty before he killed PJ and that other lady."

My scalp tingled again. She knew Helen's name. The rightful owner of the property.

"I don't know how much I can do, but I'll look into it," I said. "Why do you think someone's after you too?" She probably thought Bonnie killed Malen, which would be the precise reason they'd be after her now.

"I just have a feeling. I don't feel safe anywhere I go." Tears welled in her eyes. "I can't go back to the B&B. It reminds me too much of Malen."

Penelope oinked at my feet. I knew what that darling little piggy with a huge heart was trying to do. She was trying to get me to invite Samantha to stay with us.

I mean, the house was big enough. I probably wouldn't even notice her there.

Penelope rubbed her head on my leg, literally nudging me.

"You could stay with us," I said. "Penelope and me." I motioned down at Penelope. "We have plenty of bedrooms."

"I couldn't," Samantha said. "That's not why I came here. I swear it's not."

I opened the door and let her in. "Come on," I said. "I'll go to the B&B and gather your things later."

She hesitated, then finally came inside.

"Pick any of the rooms upstairs except for the one with the lilac wreath on the door."

"I don't know what to say," Samantha said. "Thank you so much." She wrapped her arms around me in a giant bear hug.

"I have a yoga class in a few minutes," I said. "You can join us if you want. Or you can get some sleep. All the rooms have fresh sheets and clean towels in the bathrooms."

She smiled and wiped a tear from her eye. "I don't think I'll be able to sleep, but a shower would be good."

She started up the stairs, then stopped midway up and turned back. "Thanks for looking into the case."

"Just for the record," I said. "I don't think Bonnie did it."

She shrugged and continued up the stairs.

As I was closing the door, I noticed Samantha's fancy car. PJ probably bought that for her. If he and I had stayed together, would he have bought me a car like that? Would I have wanted a car like that over Mona?

No. Definitely not.

Plus, I couldn't have stayed with him. He cheated. And had recently passed away.

I closed the door and laughed at my choice of men. I'd gone after cheaters, commitment-phobes, and murderers. Not that Ty and I had actually dated. But when I'd first seen him in the towel, I thought there'd been a spark.

That's when I remembered Ty had only just killed his uncle when I'd arrived. The towel situation had distracted me. Ugh.

See? Bad taste in men.

That was me.

7

F ocus was a challenge during yoga. Not only because I was deciding how I would go about investigating a crime that had nothing to do with me. But also because the women were restless. All they wanted to do was talk, which I tried to stop about a dozen times, then gave up.

By the time the session was over, I was the only one still doing the poses at all.

As I lay in corpse pose with my eyes closed, I listened to the chatter.

"You think Samantha is setting you up?" Nancy asked Bonnie. "But wasn't that girl her friend? She seemed pretty broken up about it."

"She's manipulative and determined to get her hands on that property," Bonnie whispered. I'd let them in on the fact that Samantha was staying with me. She hadn't come down for yoga, but I had heard the water running for a shower.

60

"If I'm out of the way, she gets the property," Bonnie said. "Ellie convinced me to go talk to the police about it. Even though they'll probably think I did it."

"Maybe Samantha deserves it," Katie said, her voice irritated. "Maybe she wouldn't completely demolish it."

"Oh, she would," Bonnie said. "But instead of trying to do what's best for the town, she'd make it into an abomination. A resort. A mall. A waterpark."

"What's best for the town?" Katie's voice was getting angrier.

Penelope nudged my ear with her snout as if to tell me I needed to jump in. But I didn't want to jump in. I just wanted to lay there holding onto the snippets of peace I could.

"Yes," Bonnie said. "What's best for the town."

"I don't think what's best for the town is demolishing Helen's Hardware to put up some gaudy chain store." Katie was getting worked up, her arms flailing all over the place. "I don't think what's best for the town is to take out one of the oldest farms in the area to build luxury houses that no one in the town could even imagine affording. I don't think what's best for the town is some hoity-toity builder coming in here and changing everything about it."

I wiggled my fingers and toes, slowly bringing my body back in line with my thoughts.

"I may be hoity-toity, but at least I don't act like I'm Cliff Haven royalty," Bonnie yelled.

Amy and Nancy gasped.

"Now that's enough." Fran thankfully stepped in so I

didn't have to. "You both think you know what's best. No offense, Bonnie, but Katie is practically queen of Cliff Haven. She's been here since she was born and is much beloved." Fran turned her attention on a blushing Katie. "And Katie, maybe Bonnie's ideas aren't all that bad."

Katie's happy face dropped. "She's not your neighbor, Fran," Katie said. "She won't take away your beautiful view of the uninterrupted sunsets. Her monstrosities won't ruin your property values."

"Monstrosities?" Bonnie looked aghast. "I think I've had enough."

She walked toward me.

"Are we going to go to the police station or not?"

I stood. "Let me get changed."

The police station sat just on the outskirts of town and was only big enough to have a small jail and dispatch center. When we walked in, it smelled like recently waxed floors and vanilla that came from a candle on the receptionist's desk.

"Hi there," I said. "We're here to see the chief."

"And you are?"

She probably knew who I was, but she looked at Bonnie when she asked the question.

"My name is Ellie Vanderwick, and this is Bonnie Carter. She has some information she'd like to give Jake about a crime committed last night."

The receptionist didn't look even slightly surprised.

She called back to Jake and then told us to meet him in his office, pointing down a small hallway.

Two men were in Jake's office—Jake and Trent. They each had a cup of coffee in their hands and easy smiles on their faces.

Until they saw Bonnie.

Jake frowned. Trent smiled.

"I thought we'd have to come looking for you," Jake said to Bonnie.

"Ellie convinced me to come in," she said. "But I'm innocent. I didn't kill anyone. I didn't even know she was dead until I talked to Ellie this morning."

"Why would you come to the Cliff Haven Police Department?" Trent said.

"Ellie and Jake are friends," Bonnie said. "And I thought Jake would be open to hearing what I have to say." She looked at me. "At least, that's what Ellie said."

"I'd like to think we are *all* open to hearing what people have to say," Trent said.

"Why don't we go into the meeting room so we can all sit down," Jake said. His office only had two chairs. Bonnie and I stood side-by-side smashed in the doorway.

Bonnie and Trent walked in front of Jake and me. Apparently, Trent had been here a few times. The benefits of being the chief's cousin.

"I appreciate you getting her to come in," Jake whispered. "Trent and I were just talking about heading out to her farm."

"I don't think she did it."

"Do you have a feeling?" Jake asked. Esme had often

helped him with cases using feelings she got about them. I'd gotten a couple the last time around, but they were all very confusing, and some were better than others. I hadn't quite learned how to hone the talent—or magic—whatever you wanted to call it.

"No feeling," I said. "But Bonnie makes a pretty compelling argument. I just hope your cousin hears her out."

"He told you?" He laughed.

I nodded. "He knew Emily too?"

"He came to visit every summer," Jake said. "He grew up in Des Moines but always liked the farm life. I suspected he had a thing for Emily too, but in the end, I won. And then lost."

My heart broke for him all over again. It brought up all kinds of different emotions and made my scalp feel like sparks were flying through each strand of hair.

"I didn't know your family had a farm," I said, changing the subject. It was too hard to talk about Emily and how she'd practically vanished from Cliff Haven.

"Yep, on the opposite side of town as yours," he said. "It's technically my farm now. After Mom and Dad passed a few years back, they left it to me."

"Were your sisters mad?" Jake often talked about his sisters and nieces and nephews.

"One got the beach house, and the other got the mountain house. It worked out for all of us."

"Do your sisters live around here?" I knew we weren't related, but some part of me couldn't let that go.

"No," he said. "But they come back for the holidays and bring all their kids with them."

A strong sense of yearning plopped into my stomach. I wanted a family Thanksgiving. A family Christmas. With people who were actually my family.

But the only people I knew were for sure my family were Esme and Emily. Esme was dead, and Emily—well—no one knew what happened to Emily.

Jake glanced up at my hair. "You okay?"

The tingling should have alerted me, but I was stuck in my feelings. "Fine," I said, pushing the dark cloud away and seeking out the sunshine. "I'm good." I smiled.

Jake smiled back and held the door open to the drab meeting room. About twenty chairs surrounded a huge table where I guessed the officers met at shift changes to discuss what had happened the previous shift.

Bonnie and Trent sat at the end closest to the door. Jake took a seat next to Trent, and I sat on the other side of the table next to Bonnie.

"Go ahead," Trent said to Bonnie, jumping right in. He already had his pen and paper ready.

"Last night, I was at the bowling alley when I saw Ellie winning." She looked over and smiled at me. "I had no idea she was so good at bowling."

I shrugged. Neither did I.

"I was standing next to the arcade games when Malen approached me to tell me about how developing the property wasn't as easy as I thought."

Trent nodded and took down some notes.

"And then everything went black, and the next thing I knew, I was parked in my driveway with ripped clothes and a serious headache."

"So when you say everything went black, are you talking about the power failure?" Trent asked.

"At first, it was just the lights." She frowned. "Then my consciousness. I think someone knocked me out."

"Did you see anyone?" Jake asked. "Or feel anything?"

"It was just Malen and me." She rubbed her arm again. "Before Ellie told me she was dead, I thought Malen might have attacked me."

"When did you wake up in your car?" Trent asked.

"Early this morning," she said.

"Let's go back a bit," Trent said. "You went to the bowling alley alone and weren't bowling, right?"

"I heard Katie and them talking about it on our walk yesterday morning," she said. "I thought it sounded like fun."

"But you didn't want to play?" Jake asked.

"I wanted to play." Bonnie looked down at her hands. "But Katie wouldn't let me."

I sighed. I needed to talk to Katie about playing nice in the sandbox with the new kids.

"Why wouldn't Katie let you play?" Jake asked.

"She hates me," Bonnie said. "Just like most of the people in town."

"Why do most of the people in town hate you?" Trent asked, looking from Bonnie to Jake.

"Remember the case we had a few weeks ago, right?" Jake asked.

"The multiple homicide?" Trent asked, glancing at me.

Bonnie's eyes glazed over in tears. Sometimes I forgot she'd just lost her son and boyfriend. If she and Samantha

66

could have gotten along, they might have been able to sympathize with each other on their losses.

"Well," Jake continued. "When the dust settled, and everyone was either dead or in jail, Bonnie ended up getting the property at the center of the case."

"Ah," Trent said. "I remember now. You also got the hardware store and a huge development company, right?"

"And it doesn't help that I'm planning on developing the cornfield into luxury living and a recreation and event center." Bonnie nodded. "At least I was, but it sounds like the property isn't even developable."

"This may be a strange question, and I don't mean to freak you out by asking you this," Trent said. "But do you think perhaps you were the target of the attack, and Malen just ended up in the crosshairs?"

Bonnie's eyes widened. "You think someone was trying to kill me?"

"It's not out of the question," Trent said.

"I thought you would say I killed her," Bonnie said. "That's why I was so afraid to talk to you about this."

"Did you kill her?" Trent's question nearly gave me whiplash.

"No—I—no," Bonnie said, obviously as taken aback by his question as I was. "Why would I come here if I killed her?"

Trent didn't return the smile. "It happens," he said. "But for now, there is not nearly enough evidence to take you into custody."

Bonnie slouched slightly in her chair, obviously relieved.

"If you think of anything else, please let us know."

Trent handed her a business card. "As for you, Miss Vanderwick, I'd like to speak with you alone if you have a moment."

"Of course," I said.

Jake led Bonnie out of the room. Trent looked up at me from his notes.

"Jake is pretty adamant that you have a knack for solving crimes," he said.

"I don't know that I'd call it a knack," I said, Jake's words hitting my heart like a ball of warmth. "Maybe I'm just observant."

"Your grandmother had a knack," Trent said.

I nodded.

"But," his tone turned more serious. "Knacks, feelings, dare I say—magic—don't hold up in court. They're not actual evidence."

He sat back and studied me before continuing.

"Esme's feelings could be a blessing but also a curse because finding evidence—solid evidence—to back them up was a challenge. And could cause a person to go looking for evidence that wasn't there. Creating evidence to support these feelings."

My head tingled a bit. I hated being reprimanded—hated confrontation—and that's exactly what this felt like.

"Jake and your grandmother had a great relationship, even after what happened with Emily." He paused. "But her input put many of his cases in jeopardy. Therefore, I'll tell you one more time to stay out of this case."

The words hit harder than I expected. I knew they were coming. I could feel it. Maybe with the same type of feeling Esme used to get. The type that jeopardized cases.

68

Trent stood. "Thank you for bringing Bonnie in. Her details of the evening fit within what we believe happened."

He may have told me to stay out of it, but I knew at that moment I wouldn't be able to. Sure, I'd stay away from Trent, but I'd promised two people I'd look into it, and I wasn't one to go back on my word.

8

On my days off from the café, I usually spent most of my time with Penelope. Our newest project was cleaning out the old barn so I could make it into a studio. At the rate we were going, it would be years before it was done. But every little bit helped.

I checked in on Samantha before we headed out to work on the barn. She was completely passed out in the brightly colored Rainbow room. The flowery bedspread covered most of her body, besides her head and one foot sticking out the side. I left the sandwich I'd made on her nightstand next to a lamp with a bright blue lampshade and tip-toed out.

Mona—my microbus—lived in the super-tidy garage. It had a brand-new cement floor, was heated, and completely clutter-free.

But the barn was a mess. When I opened the door, dust flew everywhere. Little particles floated in the air like tiny fairy lights. Penelope ran around trying to catch them in her cute little piggy mouth.

A tractor that looked older than dirt sat right in the middle. I'd been trying to find parts to make it run again, but I was no mechanic. Sure, I'd worked on Mona a bit over the years, but she was pretty simple. Heck, I'd even swapped out an engine on the side of the road once.

Some might say the engine is the heart of the vehicle, but Mona's heart was in her steering wheel. I could feel it when I drove. That steering wheel—stainless steel with tiny lilac flowers etched in—would never be replaced.

"Let's work on getting all the trash out," I said to Penelope, who spun in an excited circle.

Old boards with nails poking out littered the floor and were covered in some instances by mounds of dirt, hay, and other—slightly less appealing—elements. I suspected at one time Esme had some sheep or horses or maybe even cows.

I could picture the farm as Esme had it. As the mural in the back of the barn showed. Tidy, fresh, and surrounded by flowers and animals. In the mural, the people—three to be exact—changed. Just another example of a magic I didn't understand.

Emily—my mother—had painted the mural. Her signature was at the bottom. The first time Penelope led me to the back of the barn, three women had been in the painting. Three white-haired women. I assumed they were Esme, Emily, and me. But since then, the three women hadn't been in the picture together again. They'd each made an appearance—always looking away from me—but never all three together.

Currently, the mural was empty of people. But it had animals. Horses, goats, pigs, sheep, cows, and chickens. The image made me smile.

Penelope and I worked on the barn for well over three hours before we were both famished.

"How about a snack?" I asked my sweet little piggy friend.

Penelope squealed in excitement and dashed toward the house.

I trotted after her, happy to move my legs in a manner that didn't include squatting.

When I opened the door, the smell of something delicious hit my nose.

I peeked into the kitchen to find Katie and Nancy tending pots on the stove.

"What are the two of you doing here?" I asked playfully.

"Oh, I hope you don't mind. Samantha let us in," Nancy said. "We wanted to make you some mashed potatoes so you could start training. The race is only a couple of days away."

Which meant Thanksgiving was only a couple of days plus a couple more away.

My scalp cooled in a slow tingle sending a chill all the way down my back.

Nope.

I pushed my feelings away.

How could I feel sad when I had two wonderful women cooking one of my favorite foods in my kitchen?

"Where is Samantha?" I asked.

"She said she had to go into town for something," Nancy said. "She seems like a nice girl."

"I think she is," I said.

"Nancy and I each made a recipe. You can decide whose is best," Katie said, getting back to the task at hand.

Nancy winked. "I think they're both equally good."

"Speak for yourself," Katie said, nudging Nancy with her elbow.

They both laughed.

"I'm sure I'll love them both," I said. "And Penelope looks excited too."

"We made some special for Miss Penny," Nancy said. She was the only one who called Penelope Penny. Bex called her Bits, as in Bacon Bits. And everyone else just called her Penelope.

"Now," Katie said. "We need you to go on a run."

"A run?" I asked.

Though my legs could probably handle it, my stomach might collapse in on itself. The sandwich I had for lunch had long since digested.

"Yes," Katie said. "A run. You have to run before you eat the potatoes, or else it won't do any good."

I sighed. From the looks on their faces, they wouldn't give in. If I wanted those delicious potatoes, I would have to run first.

"And don't short change it," Nancy said. "Run the entire five kilometers."

Three miles wasn't bad when it came to running. But on an empty stomach, it would seem like running across the entire state of Iowa.

"The sooner you go, the sooner you get potatoes." Katie held up a spoonful of the golden mashed deliciousness.

"Fine," I said. "I just need to get my shoes on."

I laced up my running shoes and pulled my hair into a tight ponytail.

"We'll time you," Nancy said, excited. "Ready, set, go."

I ran out of the house and headed down the route I always took during our early morning 5k walk-runs.

The route led me past Bonnie's house and into town, around the square and back again.

When I reached the square, I waved at Bex, who was closing up the café, and Jake, who patrolled through town. I did a double-take when I saw Samantha and Trent sitting outside on one of the benches talking. So that's what she had to do in town. From the looks of things, Samantha was very emphatic in what she was telling him.

When Samantha saw me, she raised an eyebrow then went back to talking to Trent. Maybe she didn't need my help. If she and Trent were on such good terms, he could probably help her out more than I could.

I ran back down the highway for a short jaunt before taking the dirt roads back past Bonnie's and up to my front steps.

Nancy waited with a huge Tupperware bowl of mashed potatoes.

"Eat them as fast as you can," Katie said. "And don't throw up."

I took a breath. I'd run pretty hard. Probably because I was practically starving. But as delicious as the potatoes

74

sounded before the run, they looked rather unappealing now.

"Come on, eat." Nancy glanced at the stopwatch. "You're going to lose."

I wanted to remind her that I wasn't actually competing against anyone but thought it was better just to do as she said.

I shoveled those potatoes into my mouth like my life depended on it. My stomach wasn't happy. My throat was on fire—they hadn't exactly cooled while I was running.

"Come on, come on," Katie said. "Get it all in there."

Penelope even cheered with her happy squeal, though she probably didn't know exactly why they were so excited.

I took the last bite and felt like I might hurl everywhere.

"Do not throw up," Katie said. "You have to keep it down for ten minutes."

She must have seen my face turning green. Or maybe my hair was changing. I couldn't tell. All the feeling in my extremities was gone. I could only feel my stomach. And it didn't feel good.

I dropped the spoon into the tub and sat down on the porch, swallowing the last bit with a gag.

"So?" I asked when my mouth was free of potatoes. "How did I do?"

Katie showed Nancy the stopwatch, and they both smiled.

"You got this in the bag."

I kept the potatoes down well past the ten minutes.

"Now, we just have to decide which potatoes to use," Nancy said. "The ones you ate were mine. They stayed down pretty well."

"But, these are mine." Katie handed me another bowl of potatoes.

My stomach grumbled in objection.

"I don't think I can eat any more potatoes."

"Just one bite to decide on taste," Katie said. "Or we can come back tonight, and you can do this all over again."

I did not want to do it over again.

I took a bite.

"They're both tasty," I said. "Either would be great."

Katie and Nancy looked pleased by my answer. How did they expect me to choose between the two? That would be like choosing between Mona and Penelope. It wasn't possible.

"Looks like we'll be making a whole boatload of potatoes."

"Next training will be tomorrow afternoon," Katie said. "Maybe you shouldn't spend so much time in the barn using up all of your energy."

"What are you doing out in the barn, anyway?" Nancy asked.

"I'm trying to get it cleaned up so I can put a studio in there," I said.

Nancy and Katie exchanged a look.

"What?" I asked. "I know that look. It only means trouble."

"We can help," Katie said. "We're strong old ladies."

"No, I couldn't ask—"

"You didn't ask," Nancy interrupted me. "We offered. Now let's go take a look."

I hesitated. I'd only shared the mural unintentionally with Jake. I wasn't sure I was ready to share it with others.

"How about we work on it tomorrow," I said. "I have a few things I need to get done today."

"Ooh, like things about the case?" Nancy asked, her jolly red cheeks round with a smile. "Bonnie totally did it."

"I don't think she did," I said. "She hasn't told me the complete truth about what happened that night, but . . ." I paused. "Speaking of that night." I turned to Katie. "Did you tell Bonnie she couldn't bowl with you?"

Katie huffed. "It was a league. You can't just drop in on people's leagues."

"She could have hung out with you," I said. "Instead of standing in the corner."

Nancy's gaze was on the floor. She wasn't about to contradict Katie.

"You know, it's not nice to bully people," I said as gently as I could.

"Bully?" Katie gasped. "You think I'm a bully?"

I shook my head. "I don't. I think you're one of the sweetest, kindest, most wonderful women I've ever met," I said. "But I think you could be nicer to Bonnie."

"But she—"

"Yes, she wants to develop the property. That's what she does. Telling her not to would be like telling you not to put on the annual Christmas play."

"Which you'll be in, right?" Katie asked.

"Don't change the subject," I said. "But no. I'm not an actress, and I can't carry a tune."

"If I'm nicer, will you at least audition?" Katie asked.

I laughed. "If you're nicer to Bonnie, I promise to audition. But you won't like what you see or hear."

Nancy finally looked up and smiled. "You could always help me with the refreshments."

"Or lights, or sound board," Katie added. "There are so many things to do with the play."

I waved a hand. "Let's get through one holiday before we move onto Christmas," I said. "I'm starting to worry I won't love mashed potatoes anymore once this next week is over."

"One more training run," Katie said. "Then the real thing."

"Deal," I said.

"There are chocolate chip cookies for you in the refrigerator," Nancy said as they packed up all their cooking supplies. "Pop a couple in the microwave if you like them hot."

I could have cried.

Chocolate chip cookies were my weakness. I loved mashed potatoes, but they didn't hold a candle to the mighty chocolate chip cookie. My stomach might even tolerate a cookie or two.

I hugged both of them tight. "Thank you."

"Esme would never forgive us if we didn't take care of you as if you were our own," Nancy said.

"Plus, we kinda like you." Katie winked.

Penelope oinked up at the fridge as if to say, let's eat the cookies now.

I walked the women out and then returned to the kitchen. Penelope and I ate at least half of the cookies straight from the fridge, sitting on the red brick kitchen floor.

9

I didn't know where to start with the investigation. It wasn't like I knew Malen. I mean, I knew she was a terrible belly dancer, had a husband she despised, and friends who sobbed uncontrollably when she died. She was an attorney but was being taken off Samantha's case and replaced by her soon-to-be ex-husband.

It came down to talking to Bex if I wanted to get anywhere.

Bex ran the café in the mornings but kept busy helping around town doing odds and ends in the afternoon. Sometimes she walked people's dogs, others she decorated the square for various holidays. She and her friends were currently working on getting the town ready for the Trot 'n Tater.

The sun was getting low in the sky, and the bare trees in the square let the sun streak the pavement with its golden hues. I glanced around, but Samantha and Trent were no longer sitting on their bench chatting. She still hadn't come back to the house, but I wasn't her mother. I didn't need to keep tabs on her.

"Hey, Ellie," Bex said when I hopped out of Mona's driver's side door. She had on her signature bell-bottoms and an oversized sweatshirt from a previous Trot 'n Tater. "Can you grab those cones and bring them over here?"

Bex wasn't shy about ordering people around. Most of the time, she did it in the nicest manner possible.

Most of the time.

I picked up the cones—purple in color—and took them to what looked like the finish line directly in the middle of the square, next to the gazebo.

"You can just set them there." She pointed to where I was standing. "They'll make up the finisher's chute."

I dropped the cones and brushed the dirt from them off my hands.

"Just think, you'll probably be the first one to see those cones." Bex was decorating the gazebo with fall leaves and what looked like strings of lights, even though the event was during the day. "I hear you're very fast."

"And I hear there are lots of people who run this race," I said. "I might be able to beat Katie and the others, but real runners will absolutely win over me."

Bex waved a hand as if she didn't believe me. "You never give yourself enough credit."

I blushed. "Thanks," I said. "But I wanted to ask you about—"

"Samantha?" Bex laughed. "I figured it was just a matter of time."

"Well, yes, Samantha and her attorney—Malen."

"From what I've gathered, you're not supposed to be

poking your nose into this case." She arranged and rearranged some decorations, stood back and looked, then went back to rearranging.

"Trent told you?"

"He's practically told the whole town," she said. "He thinks he can bring his big-city-boy energy into our little town and tell us what to do? He may be related to Jake, but that doesn't mean he can tell me who to talk to and who not to."

I smiled. "So you will talk to me?"

"Course I will." She brushed a black curl from her face. "What do you need to know?"

"I suppose I need to know anything you know about Malen."

"She was staying at Belinda's." Bex nodded her head toward the B&B. "Which isn't surprising since the B&B is the only place to stay in town. She and Samantha were sharing a room, from what Belinda told me."

"They didn't seem like the type to share rooms," I said. "I'm sure they could have afforded their own rooms."

Bex shrugged. "The B&B is probably pretty busy right now with the holiday and the race and all."

"Do you know if her husband or her other friends are staying there too?"

"The other women are, yes," Bex said. "I'm not sure about the husband. What's his name?"

"Chad," I replied. "I think he's been in town a couple of days. He was at the bowling alley, but you might not have noticed him."

"The guy who got the drink thrown in his face?"

"That's the one."

"I haven't seen him anywhere but the bowling alley," Bex said. "Do you think he's a suspect?"

"If I go by the TV shows, the spouse is always a suspect." I laughed. "I know everyone thinks Bonnie killed Malen, but I think the police need to look into Chad. Malen seemed so irritated when he showed up at the bowling alley and when she died, he was nowhere to be found."

"Sounds like a good lead," she said. "You and Samantha seem to be getting along. Is it weird that you both dated the same guy?"

"Not really," I said. "Even though he was one of my longest relationships, when it was over, it was over."

"Why'd you break up?"

"He cheated, I freaked, my hair changed." I shrugged. "And then when he came into town to claim his rights to the farm, he took me out for dinner, making it seem like a date, before telling me he was engaged and was only there for a business deal."

"Ouch," she said. "Men suck sometimes."

"It's about par for the course for me." I twirled a perfectly white piece of hair around my finger. "If it wasn't for my crazy hair, maybe that would be different."

"Don't discount your hair," Bex said. "No one in town is afraid of it."

"No one in town is young and single either," I said.

"Tell me about it," Bex laughed and stood back to admire her handiwork. "How does it look?"

"It looks wonderful," I said. She'd done a beautiful job. "What can I do to help?"

She contemplated this for a moment. "Can you help Beth with the park benches?"

I sucked in a breath.

Bex gave me a sideways grin.

"Sure," I said.

"I think it'll help the two of you get to know one another better."

"Whatever you think."

I meandered over to where Beth was decorating the park benches in more fake leaves and lights. Even I had to admit they looked nice.

"What do you want?" Beth asked when she saw me approaching. She had on a pair of navy cargo pants and a white t-shirt under an oversized black jacket. Her hair was back in a low ponytail and covered by a knit hat.

I was probably the only person in the world who instantly thought someone was hiding the color of their hair when they wore a hat. When I was younger, I'd look very closely at any hat-covered hair, hoping I'd find someone else with the same problem as me. But my efforts never came to fruition.

"Bex sent me over to help," I said to Beth. "What can I do?"

"Wave your magic wand and get all these lights strung around the benches."

I couldn't tell if she was joking. I picked up a strand of lights and started wrapping.

"Sorry," Beth said in a small voice. "That wasn't nice."

I shrugged and smiled at her. "It's okay. I understand."

"I hear you're trying to figure out who killed that girl at the bowling alley."

"Officially, I'm staying out of it."

"And unofficially?" Beth asked.

I looked around, halfway expecting Trent to be hiding behind a tree listening. "I'm just asking some questions."

"Who do you think did it?"

Beth may have been acting nice, but I knew she didn't like me. Which was enough for me to keep things a bit closer to the vest, so to speak.

"I don't know," I said. "With the last investigation, I accused a lot of people who didn't do it. I'd like to avoid doing that again."

Beth nodded. "It's probably the husband."

"Why?" I asked.

"Isn't it always the husband?"

She laughed, and I joined in.

"There." She stood back from the bench. "How does that look?"

I looked over at her bench to find a perfectly threaded string of lights and fake leaves. I didn't even need to look back at mine to know it looked like verifiable poop compared to hers.

"It looks fantastic," I said. "You're very talented."

She shrugged. "It's probably why all of my friends want me as their maid of honor." Beth sighed. "Being the maid of honor is exhausting with all the bachelorette plans, the party favors, the picking up the event planner's slack."

"Maybe you should go into event planning or decorating," I said. "You seem to have a gift for it."

Beth looked at me with wide eyes. "I have a really secure job. I couldn't just leave it."

"I get that," I said. "I guess the question would be, who will you choose for your maid of honor when the time comes?"

Beth laughed. "If the time comes, you mean."

"I'm sure you'll find someone someday." I re-wrapped the lights, trying to make them look like Beth's.

"That's easy for you to say, you're beautiful."

I could feel a blush rising up my neck and into my scalp.

Beth flinched when she looked at my hair.

"And that's the biggest problem I have," I said. "Most men don't exactly stick around when they find out my hair has a mind of its own."

Beth moved onto the next bench. "Why can't you control it?"

"No clue," I said. "I've never been able to."

"Maybe I do have a better chance than you," she said, but there was no humor in her voice. She may have been being nice to me, but I could still sense the animosity there. "Even if there's no way I'll find someone in this podunk town."

"I've noticed there aren't many single men in Cliff Haven."

"Nope," Beth said. "If you didn't marry a guy right out of high school or college, the chances are good you'll die alone."

"Or find someone somewhere else?" I asked. It seemed rather drastic to accept your lonely death at such a young age.

Beth shrugged. "I'll work on the ones over there. Don't mess these up too badly."

I looked at the one I'd just finished. It wasn't pretty. But at least there were lights on the bench.

———

I worked on the benches for about two more hours, stopping in the middle to drink some cocoa Katie brought over from the café.

"What are you doing for Thanksgiving?" Bex asked me when the group of us huddled in the gazebo with hot drinks cupped in our hands.

I shrugged. "I'll probably make a nice little dinner for Penelope and me. We love watching the parade on TV and maybe some football too."

"That sounds fun," she said, but her tone didn't sound like she thought it sounded fun.

I thought I saw Beth and another girl laugh out of the corner of my eye. I guess it was too much to hope that the bit of conversation we had might have changed things between us.

"What are you doing?" I asked, ignoring them.

"Deb always has Thanksgiving at her house. Mom and Dad will come too," she said. Deb was her sister and a Cliff Haven Police Officer. "I'll probably be in charge of the stuffing."

"Mmmm stuffing," I said. "Do you run the Trot 'n Tater?"

"Heck no," Bex laughed. "Not all black girls can run, you know."

I laughed too. "Or play basketball?" I teased.

"Or sing." She rolled her eyes. "You wouldn't believe

how many times the choir director at school thought she'd give me a solo, only to remember I can't carry a tune to save my life."

I laughed. "That makes two of us."

"That confirms it, then," Bex said, wrapping an arm around my shoulder.

"Confirms what?"

"That we were meant to be best friends."

"I don't know how Beth will take the news," I whispered, glancing at Beth. Thankfully, she was in a conversation with Katie and the other women.

"Beth and I are only friends because it's always been that way. You'll find out when you live in a small town long enough, people don't rock the boat. We've been friends since elementary school, so we'll always be friends." She squeezed my shoulder. "But you—I choose you to be my friend. Which means you're the best one."

"I'm honored," I said, trying to keep my voice from choking up.

1 0

W

e worked until it started to get dark. Bex said goodnight as she and the others headed to their cars on the opposite side of the square as Mona.

When I opened Mona's door, something was off. Something was different. Someone had been in my van. Or around my van. Or messed with my van. Something.

"What is it, Mona?" I asked, reaching for the steering wheel.

My hair tingled, frizzing up almost like I'd been electrocuted.

Mona was distressed. I could feel it through the wheel.

I looked underneath but saw nothing out of the ordinary.

This was one of the feelings I couldn't push away. I'd pushed away a feeling of danger once before because I thought it was embarrassment.

I slid into the seat and closed the door.

With both hands on the wheel, I concentrated. What

was the feeling trying to tell me? What was Mona trying to tell me?

My hair buzzed aloud now. At least, I felt like it was aloud. I could hear it.

Then all at once, my mind came into focus, and the buzzing stopped.

Someone had messed with Mona's wiring.

I hugged Mona's wheel. "It's okay. I'll fix it."

She seemed more at peace.

The engine was in the back of the bus, something that many people didn't know. Something I didn't realize until I'd had my first round of engine trouble only days after my seventeenth birthday.

I opened the hatch and turned on my phone flashlight.

The wires looked like they'd been tampered with, but none were cut. More like they were just out of place.

I searched some more but found nothing that seemed to be dangerous.

When I got back into the driver's seat, I grabbed the steering wheel again, but everything seemed like it was back to normal. Mona was okay.

I sighed. Maybe my feelings weren't always right. Maybe the danger I sensed had to do with something else.

I glanced around the square. All the shops were closed. White lights spiraled down light posts, adding a twinkling glow to the fog settling into town. There wasn't a soul to be found.

Or was there?

A shadow I had to have glanced over before practically jumped out and smacked me in the forehead.

Someone crouched next to the gazebo, staring in my direction.

I knew better than to approach a strange figure. I considered calling Jake, but what if he thought I was over-reacting? I didn't want to be the squeaky wheel that eventually everyone stopped listening to.

If someone wanted to stalk around in the shadows, then I'd let them. Heck, maybe it was a couple of teenagers afraid they'd get caught kissing in the bushes.

My hair was telling me it wasn't innocent. Not entirely, anyway. It wasn't that my hair was warning me of danger, but it wanted me to know someone was there.

I pushed the thoughts away. Just because someone was hiding in the bushes didn't mean they were a criminal.

Unless they were.

Ugh. Stop. My brain wouldn't shut off.

As I turned the corner to head out of town, the figure emerged, and a chill ran up my neck and through the very ends of my hair.

A stunningly gorgeous man stared at me. He wore all black. Black jeans, a black t-shirt, and a black leather jacket, all of which accentuated his muscular build. He completed the look with black boots and shoulder-length black hair.

I kept moving. The guy threw his hands in the air as if he was waving me down. I slowed and pulled the pepper spray I'd kept in the pouch hanging on the dash for times like this. Just because he was cute didn't mean he wasn't dangerous.

I watched him approach in my side mirror, a weird look on his face.

Why had I stopped?

I could have just hit the gas and taken off. But that would have been rude. So rude. And maybe he just had one of those resting grumpy faces.

I cracked the window with one hand and held the pepper spray can in my other with a finger on the trigger.

"Can I help you?" I asked.

"How did you do that?" He ran a hand over the stubble covering his chin. He was probably a couple of years older than me, with deeply tanned skin and huge green eyes.

"Do what?" I asked, stumbling over my words. Whether I couldn't speak was because he was hot or because I was so on edge was beyond me.

"How did you fix your van so fast?"

I looked down at Mona's wheel, bringing my thoughts back into reality. The last thing I needed to do was check out a bad boy. Regardless of how cute he was.

"I didn't fix anything," I said. "Nothing was wrong with it." Then it hit me. "Did you try to break Mona?"

He laughed a hoarse laugh. "Mona?"

"It's her name," I said, trying not to sound too indignant. "Why would you hurt my van?"

"I didn't," he said. "But that other person—the one in the park earlier—did."

"One of the ones I was decorating with?" I asked.

"Not the ones who made the park benches completely unusable," he said. "The one who was watching you."

"Man? Woman? Child?" I was getting frustrated. It sounded like this guy had messed with Mona—unsuccessfully, of course—and was making people up. Plus, I'd had a long day. I was ready to cozy up in my bed with Penelope.

"I don't know. They kept their hood up the entire time." He looked confused. "I thought you were a witch. What witch doesn't notice when someone is stalking her?"

"Who are you?" I asked, ready to pepper spray him just for assuming I was a witch. Which, who knew, maybe I was. But that wasn't for him to decide.

"Xander." He reached a couple of fingers through the window to shake my hand.

I hesitantly reached up and met his fingers with mine. A bolt of electricity stole through me when our fingers touched. It wasn't unpleasant, but it made every hair on my body want to stand on end.

I yanked my hand away and tried to determine if he'd felt it too. Either he hadn't, or he was a great actor because his face was still the same.

"Uh, I'm—"

"Ellie Vanderwick," he said. "I know. Everyone knows."

Everyone? Surely, not everyone knew.

"So you saw someone mess with Mona, and you did nothing about it? You were just going to watch me get blown up?"

He laughed again. "You weren't going to blow up. If anything, she wouldn't have started. They just cut some wires."

I shook my head. "There were no cut wires. I checked."

He studied me as if I might be lying. Then shrugged. "Okay, if you say so."

"After this person supposedly cut the wires, what did they do?"

"They disappeared," he said. "Poof."

"Okay," I said. "I'm leaving."

I put Mona in drive.

"Wait, don't go."

But I was already going. That guy was freaking me out. People didn't disappear. No magic in this world just made people disappear.

Before heading home, I drove to the B&B to retrieve Samantha's belongings as I promised. The teenage girl working at the desk barely took down my name before handing me a key.

The B&B was delightful. It was modeled after an old farmhouse but had lots of fun and quirky updates. Samantha and Malen's room was a total disaster. It was hard to differentiate between what was Samantha's and what was Malen's. But I figured if I accidentally added some of Malen's things, Samantha could get them sorted out.

The queen-size bed sat in the middle of the room, and a window seat provided a view overlooking the town.

Once I felt confident I had most of Samantha's items in the blue bag she instructed me to get, I gave the room a once over. I knew I should have just left. There was no reason I needed to snoop around.

Except for the fact that I was supposed to be looking

into the case. And all of Malen's stuff was just sitting out for anyone to see.

I eased the door back into the closed position and turned the lock. Yeah, that made it feel even more wrong, but I didn't want to be caught. At least someone with a key would make enough noise for me to stop doing whatever I was doing and act natural.

Papers on the desk were an easy first target. Divorce papers. Signed by Malen, but not yet by Chad. They looked pretty typical for divorce papers. Nothing stood out. The cause of divorce was irreconcilable differences.

Dead end.

I looked under the bed but found nothing.

Malen didn't seem to have as many things with her as Samantha did. Then my eyes landed on it—her briefcase.

If there were a clue, it would be inside that briefcase.

My feet were heavy. I didn't want to open it. It wasn't right.

And yet, I needed to.

I reached out for it, and my arm went numb. Like, can't feel it at all, numb.

That was enough of a reason for me to give up.

I dropped my arm and walked away.

It was a bad idea, and I knew it.

The door handle started jiggling before I reached for it. Panic set in, making me freeze completely. My hair felt like it was singeing from the roots.

Danger echoed through every part of me. Surely my hair was bright red.

Whoever was on the other side of that door was not someone I wanted to come into contact with. I glanced around for an exit. I was on the second floor, and the windows looked like they were painted shut.

The door knob wasn't turning. The person out there obviously didn't have a key, or they would be inside by now.

I took a few deep breaths. It would be okay. But just to be certain, I moved into the bathroom, closed the door, and stepped into the tub behind the shower curtain.

Persistent knocking replaced the handle jiggling. Did they think Samantha was inside? Or maybe they didn't know Malen died? Or perhaps it was just a pushy maid?

Then a thought dawned on me. What if whoever was out there was out there for me? Was it the mysterious man from the square? Was it Xander?

I shivered.

Either way, it probably wasn't good.

Then they stopped knocking.

Silence followed, but my hair still felt like it was on fire.

The danger hadn't passed.

It wasn't a maid.

Talking myself out of my hair's warning signs was something I needed to get out of the habit of doing.

The bathroom was starting to fog. I reached up and found my hair was hot to the touch. I quietly pulled back the curtain to look in the mirror, afraid I might see my hair actually burning itself up.

But the mirror was so fogged I couldn't see anything.

I stayed in the tub until my hair cooled, and I heard nothing from the hallway for who knew how long.

I stepped out and went to wipe the mirror but saw the remains of a message written there once before.

It either said, you're my world, or you're my worm. I'd guess world. And it made everything come into focus.

Malen and Samantha weren't merely friends. They were together. Hence the one room. The one bed. Samantha's reaction when she saw Malen's body.

And perhaps the reason Malen was dead, and Samantha thought someone was after her.

11

Before I headed home, I asked the teenager if anyone had come upstairs. She looked at me as if I was crazy, shook her head, and promptly shoved her headphones back over her ears. She likely wouldn't have heard anything anyway with those on.

I checked Mona over quickly before we headed home, then more thoroughly when she was safely in my garage. If someone was trying to sabotage her, I needed to keep a better eye on things. And be more aware of my surroundings.

I couldn't believe someone had been stalking me, and I hadn't even noticed. And whether that person was the one Xander talked about, or Xander himself, it was still disconcerting knowing my hair hadn't warned me of anything. At least it told me something when I'd gotten to Mona, but then again, that hadn't exactly panned out either.

I locked the garage after I was satisfied that Mona was perfectly okay and headed into the house.

I expected Samantha to be there since her car was in the driveway, but I didn't expect the entire bride brigade to be lounging all over my living room. A movie was playing on the television over the fireplace, but they weren't really paying attention. They were giggling and gossiping and doing all the things friends did.

Missy walked into the room, expertly balancing four paper plates with steaming hot pizza. "Oh sorry," Missy said. "I didn't know you'd be here."

Everyone turned to look at me.

"I can get you a slice," she said.

"I'm okay," I said.

"Come on, Ellie," Samantha said, standing from the couch. She nearly tipped over as she tried to reach for my hand. "Have pizza with us."

She was drunk.

"Where's Penelope?" I asked.

"She's right here." Janelle sat up, revealing a snoozing Penelope wrapped up in a blanket. "She's the best little piggy in the whole wide world."

I smiled. "Okay, I'll take a slice."

"Yay!" Samantha finally latched onto my arm and dragged me down onto the couch with her.

I watched the movie and devoured the pizza and pretended these women were my friends. I'd never had friends before. Not like this.

The closest I'd ever come was my foster families and the other kids. Sometimes they were nice. Sometimes we played. But it never lasted.

"Are you okay?" Samantha asked, leaning over to me.

"I just think it's sweet you guys are so close," I said,

not realized I'd been tearing up. "I bet it's been hard to deal with the loss of one of your friends."

"Hey, hey, hey," Missy said, turning to look at me. "None of that talk. We're trying to make the most of things."

"Oh sorry," I said.

Samantha dabbed a tear from her eye next to me.

"See what you did," Missy said. "It's okay, Sammy. She didn't mean to make you cry."

I thought I heard Samantha mumble, "It's Samantha," under her breath.

"Look," Missy continued. "We're stuck here. The cops don't want us going home yet. Which is fine because we had the trip booked through the weekend." She reached over and grabbed Janelle's hand. "And Janelle deserves to have her bachelorette weekend."

Janelle didn't look like she much cared to have her bachelorette weekend but seemed drunk enough to let her friend's ramblings go.

"You should have brought some of the good stuff," Becky said, giggling.

Missy shot her a look that could have withered a flower. "We don't talk about the good stuff."

"What do you mean, good stuff?" I asked. I had an idea of what they were talking about but wanted to be sure.

"Missy may have gone to college for botany," Janelle said. "But the real plant life was growing in her dorm."

Missy threw a pillow at Janelle. "Stop." At least she was smiling now. "That was a long time ago. I was a kid."

"Not that long," Becky said. "Pretty sure I saw the

same plant life in your apartment garden a couple of weeks ago."

I shook my head and laughed. At least they hadn't brought the "good stuff" into my home.

I turned to Samantha, who still looked like she might burst out into tears at any moment. "Can I ask you something?" I lowered my voice so only she could hear.

"You can ask me anything," Samantha said. "I'm the openest book in the world."

I laughed. "Were you and Malen more than friends?" I made sure my voice was so low that even Samantha might have a hard time hearing me.

"Why would you think that?" she asked, but she'd dropped her gaze to the afghan blanket draped over her lap and was threading her fingers in and out of the holes.

"Just a hunch," I said. "I went to get your stuff from your room at the B&B, and I saw a message on the mirror."

She smiled slightly. "Did you take a shower or something?"

"Something like that," I said.

The look in her eyes when she glanced back up at me was the only confirmation I needed.

"I'm sorry for your loss."

She shrugged and wiped a tear away. "That cop from the other town—Trent—doesn't think I have anything to worry about. He thinks this might have been a random attack."

I raised my eyebrows.

"Yeah, that's what I thought too."

"I don't want to freak you out," I said. "But when I

was at your room at the B&B, someone was trying to get it. They were banging at the door and everything."

Her eyes widened. "Who do you think it was?"

"I don't know," I said. "But let's just say I have a feeling whoever it was wasn't there for a friendly visit."

"So, you *are* a witch?" she said, then laughed.

"If I were, I would have been able to use my powers to protect myself. Instead, I hid in the shower."

She and I both laughed at the thought of that.

"Either way," I said. "I want you to be extra careful. I don't know if they were there for you or me or even Malen if they hadn't heard, but I don't want you to get hurt."

She reached over and hugged me. "Thank you for bringing me my stuff. And for understanding about Malen and me."

"Why would you marry PJ if you loved someone else?" I asked when she released me from the hug.

"It was the expectation," she said. "My family thought I needed to marry him. Then when he died, they pretty much gave up on any hope that I'd marry up. As if PJ is the only wealthy man on the planet."

"Did they know about Malen?"

She shook her head. "I'm not ready to tell anyone."

"I get it," I said. "My lips are sealed. My eyes will be too if I don't go to bed soon."

"Wait," she said. "I have a question for you."

"Okay," I said.

"You said I could choose whichever room I wanted besides the one with the lilac wreath, right?"

"Yes."

"But all the doors were locked besides the room I'm

in," she said. "Not that I don't love it, I do. But I just didn't know why you'd want me in that specific room."

"I never locked any of the doors," I said. "That's strange."

She shrugged. "Either way, I'm glad it's the room I got. It's so pretty and cheerful. And the bed is the most luxurious thing I've ever slept on."

I specifically remember trying to sleep on the bed in the rainbow room. It had been anything but luxurious, in my opinion. "Well, I'm glad you like it."

"Thanks again for letting me stay," she said.

"Any time." I stood from the couch. "Don't stay up too late," I said in a joking voice.

Penelope heard me and followed me out of the room.

When we got to the top of the stairs, Penelope bolted off to our bedroom while I tried the handles of all the doors. Surely, I hadn't locked them.

Every single one turned, and the doors easily swung open.

It was strange, but there were probably a million possible explanations. None of which I could come up with since my brain felt like complete and total mush.

I walked into the bedroom, and Penelope was standing by the switch that led to the attic.

"Not tonight, Penelope," I said. "I'm so tired."

But she let out a squeal that could have woken the dead.

"Okay, fine." I pushed the button and slid the bookcase open.

She darted up the polished wood staircase ahead of me.

Fairy lights lit the space. I had made no changes since I'd moved in. I couldn't. It was absolutely perfect, just the way Esme had it. Windows surrounded the space, which was relatively simply decorated. A leather chair where I'd spent many hours was covered with a blanket that still smelled like lilac—what I imagined Esme smelled like—and sat next to a small wooden table.

Penelope waited patiently for me next to the chair.

When I approached, I sat down and pulled her into my lap. "Is this what you wanted?"

But she was still wiggly. She pushed her neck out to the table next to the chair and nudged Esme's journal.

"You know I can't read it," I said.

The journal had saved my life once. But when I'd finally come around to trying to read it, the words were in a language I didn't recognize. I'd tried over and over again, but I couldn't translate it.

Penelope nudged it again.

"Okay, I'll try." I opened the book gently.

The first few pages were still in the strange language.

"See? It's still the same," I said, showing Penelope the journal.

I ran a finger over the slice that tore through the cover and a few pages within. A wave of gratitude washed over me, and I could feel my hair changing.

Penelope oinked happily.

Was that what she wanted? To make me feel better?

I closed the book and went to put it back on the stand, but Penelope squealed so loudly I nearly jumped out of the chair.

"What?" I asked.

She nudged the book again, this time more forcefully.

I opened it again and turned a few more pages. There was something I needed to see in this book. Or so Penelope thought.

She was my best friend, but sometimes I had to remind myself that she was just a pig. There were probably just crumbs in the spine or something.

But deep down, I knew it wasn't that. Not only because I never ate around this book, but also because Penelope had a way of making me see things. A way of knowing. She may have just been a pig, but she was a smart little oinker.

When I landed on a page I'd seen a thousand times before, I nearly passed it. Until I realized I could read the words.

A watercolor portrait of maybe Esme or Emily was on the left page, and a couple of paragraphs were on the right. I squinted against the dim light to read.

I found her.

Not Emily.

Ellie.

I didn't know. How could I have known?

He said she's in Colorado—the man who recently arrived in town. The man who seemed to be looking for me.

The rumble of his motorcycle up the drive was a sound I hadn't heard since my younger days.

He gave me a photograph. She's beautiful, just like her mom. And I've missed so many years.

Why didn't Emily tell me? Is that why she went missing? Did she think I would be angry?

I may never know.

What I do know is, I need to find her. Now. Before it's too late.

The page was wrinkled as if it had gotten wet with teardrops. I carefully brushed my own away.

I cupped one of my curls in the palm of my hand. The tiniest bit of gold streaked through the white.

I flipped through a few more pages, but none of the others had changed to reveal their messages to me. I read over Esme's words one more time before setting the book back where it belonged.

"Thank you, Penelope," I said, snuggling her. But she was fast asleep.

12

The day of the race was cold. Not your average fall chill, it was downright nasty. The wind whipped through the trees in the square, sending most of Beth's and my hard work flying.

If Xander thought the benches were un-sittable before, he'd be happy now.

I shook my head. It was strange that Xander popped up in my thoughts. Why was I thinking about him when I should have been concentrating on the race? Maybe it was that little zap I got when our hands touched? What was that all about?

I wasn't great with men, but I knew one thing: Xander was trouble if I ever saw it.

Penelope and Bex stood at the start-finish line, yelling and squealing for me. I wrapped my arms around my body, trying to keep the cool, humid air from giving me the chills.

"Hey you," James from the bowling alley appeared

next to me, fully decked out in running attire. "I didn't know you were a runner."

My breath caught in my chest. I hadn't expected him to be here.

"I didn't know you were either," I finally said.

"I guess there's a lot we need to get to know about one another," he said.

"Ooh, what are we getting to know?" I turned to find Xander on the other side of me. He wore all black again, but instead of black boots, he wore black running shoes.

I took a step away from him, tripped on my own feet, and fell right into James' arms.

"Oh hey," James said. His eyes were gorgeous. They almost made me forget about the awkward position I was in.

"You okay?" James said, helping me back to a standing position.

"I'm fine." I glanced over at Xander, who had taken a couple of steps away. "Thanks."

"I was just telling Ellie, she and I should get to know each other," James said to Xander. "I didn't realize she thought I meant now." He laughed. "I'm James."

"Xander."

They nodded at one another as I stood there, completely mortified. Thank goodness I was wearing a hat because I knew my hair was changing. I could feel the sparks in my roots.

"How do you know Ellie, Xander?" James asked.

"I don't," Xander said. "I just know of her." He leaned toward James—across me—as if he were telling James a secret, but his voice didn't lower. "I hear she's the one to beat in this race."

James smiled and looked at me. "Is that so?"

When I glanced over at Bex and mouthed the word help, she just shrugged and laughed. Penelope, on the other hand, looked like she might jump right out of Bex's arms.

Bex held on tight to my protective little piggy.

I tried to clear my mind with a few deep breaths of cold air.

Katie was preparing to speak into the microphone from the podium on the gazebo. She wore her nicest black tracksuit, complete with a multi-colored running cape.

Nancy, Fran, Amy, and Bonnie were off to the side of the finish line, scooping gobs of steaming potatoes into clear Tupperware dishes. It made me smile to see the others taking Bonnie under their wings. Maybe there was hope for them after all.

To my right, Samantha and her friends were pushing their way to the front of the line. Samantha left the house before I woke up to have breakfast with her friends before their big race. They all wore long-sleeved t-shirts that said Janelle's Trot 'n Tater Team, sparkly pink beanie hats, and big smiles.

Well, everyone but Samantha had a big smile. Samantha looked only slightly happy. Which made sense when you considered the person she loved most in the world had just died.

"Drink up, ladies," Missy shouted, bringing Samantha's attention back to her friends. I was getting the feeling Missy was the mom of the group. "We can't get dehydrated before the big race."

They all took a sip from their special water bottles. They were a teal green this time but still had their names on them. It was a nice touch. Maybe someday I'd have fun bachelorette swag.

Samantha glanced over at me and mouthed, "Good luck."

I smiled. "You too," I said but knew she couldn't hear me.

"Are those your friends?" Xander asked.

"I guess, in a way," I said, my voice cracking from being startled. "Why?"

"No reason." But he was smiling at Becky—the shorter blonde. She blushed and smiled back.

"I would introduce you," I said. "But I'm pretty sure she's married."

"That's all right," he said. "Brunettes are more my speed."

I almost reached to my definitely-not-brunette hair but stopped myself before I gave away what I was thinking. What was I thinking? This guy was dangerous. But my hair was behaving itself. No burning.

"Hello everyone, we're so happy you could make it today!" Katie's voice blasted from the loudspeakers.

The runners around me cheered. I clapped my hands and pedaled my feet to stay warm.

"This is the largest turnout we've ever had for Cliff Haven's Annual Trot 'n Tater. We expect to have an exciting race."

More cheers.

"The rules of the race are simple," Katie said. "Stay on the marked path—you'll see the purple cones throughout the course. When you get to the finish line, you'll have your very own bucket of perfectly warmed—and delicious, I might add—mashed potatoes. The first person to finish their entire bucket of potatoes wins. But if that person vomits within ten minutes of finishing, they're disqualified, and the race will go to the next in line."

Nods all around told me many of the people had done this before. I almost turned to the men on either side of me and asked if they had, but then thought better of it. I didn't need to have a discussion right now. I needed to focus.

"Now, everyone on your mark." Katie held up a sparkly purple flag as if she was some sort of fashionable NASCAR official. "Get set." The men next to me hunched over in racing stances. "Go."

Katie quickly jumped into the race with Nancy, Bonnie, Fran, and Amy.

I paced myself but was quickly ahead of most of the group. I say most because Xander and James easily kept up with me. Samantha and her friends—besides Janelle— weren't too far behind either. Malen probably would have had me beat. The thought made me sad.

"What's wrong?" Xander asked.

"Why do you think anything's wrong?" I didn't like talking while I was running a race.

"Your hair is turning blue," he whispered.

I glanced over to see a strand of blue hair poking out of my hat. I pushed it back in.

"Maybe blue means I'm happy," I said.

"Blue never equates to happiness," he said. "Unless I'm looking in your eyes."

"Too bad I'm not a brunette, huh?" I laughed.

He shrugged. "Guess so."

"You know, you two can go ahead," I said to Xander and James. "You don't have to let me win."

"Who said we would let you win?" Xander asked, obviously out of breath.

"Well, I mean—" James started, but Xander cut him off.

"No way, man. You can't let her win."

Xander took off ahead of us, but James stayed back.

"Now that he's gone," James said. "How about we schedule a date?"

Not him too.

"Let's talk about this after the race," I said, increasing my speed. Xander was ahead, but not too far. And I was going to catch him.

I took off at a sprint. I knew my legs couldn't go this fast the entire race, but if I was careful, I could hit a good stride and be far enough ahead to beat Xander.

"Look at you," Xander said, his words coming out in staccato bursts.

"I have no intention of letting you win either," I said, passing him easily. Now, if I could just hold him off for the rest of the race.

When I was almost to the final turn that would lead to the finish line, I saw Samantha's fancy car parked in front of Belinda's B&B, and standing next to it was a man who looked like he was trying to break in.

"Hey, that's not your car," I yelled, keeping my stride.

The man turned, glared at me, and then ran off into the trees. It was Chad, Malen's husband.

I considered chasing after him, but the finish line was in sight.

I glanced behind me to see Samantha and Missy in a dead sprint. I picked up my speed and crossed the finish line only seconds before them.

Where had Xander and James gone? I searched around me.

"Don't forget about the potatoes," a volunteer shouted as if she was telling me to hurry and eat.

I raced toward the jugs of potatoes and started shoveling the warm fluffiness into my mouth.

Samantha did the same, though she seemed to have a much smaller mouth than me and was struggling a bit. Missy looked like she might vomit.

Xander and James finally appeared next to me, and then in a flash, people surrounded me, shoveling mashed potatoes into their mouths.

I ate spoonful after spoonful.

I was going to win.

I could feel it.

I took the last bite and showed the judge. Excitement flowed through me, sending sparks of joy to the tips of my hair. Thank goodness it was under a hat. Otherwise, it might have caused a scene in the middle of the square.

"We have a winner," a volunteer yelled from the podium. "Ellie Vander—"

A scream came from my right.

Everyone stopped eating.

I pushed my way through the group of people still

eating their potatoes to find Missy looking like she might pass out and Samantha laying on the ground, spoon still clutched in her hand.

I rushed to Samantha's side. "Missy, get the paramedics," I yelled.

She didn't move. She seemed to be in shock.

"Missy. Paramedics. Now."

She hesitated a split second, then sprang into action.

I tipped Samantha's head back and checked for breathing. There was no air entering her lungs.

Xander and James knelt on either side of me.

"What happened?" James asked.

"She might be choking on the potatoes," Xander said, checking for a pulse. "Or maybe not."

He retracted his fingers from her neck and interlaced them with the other hand. "Stand back. I need to give her CPR."

But something in me—a feeling deep down—knew CPR wouldn't help.

Samantha was dead.

Just like Malen.

13

The paramedics took over CPR as they loaded Samantha into the ambulance.

The mashed potato eating portion of the race completely halted. When Katie, Fran, Amy, Bonnie, and Nancy crossed the finish line hooting and hollering, the entire crowd glared at them.

Once Katie realized what was going on, she hurried to the gazebo and put holiday music on the loudspeakers, but no one seemed to appreciate the festivities.

Xander and James had walked away with the paramedics to tell them what had happened and seemed to have gotten caught up with Jake, who was probably asking them a bunch of questions. I was likely next, but while no one was watching, I surveyed the scene. Focusing on the possible crime helped me keep my thoughts off my emotions. Samantha was almost like a friend, and now she was dead. Her things were in my house.

I brushed a stray tear from my cheek.

How had she died? I looked down at the spoon she'd

been holding, but it looked like a normal spoon. The half-eaten tub of potatoes lay on the ground too. Maybe the potatoes were poisoned.

My stomach was full, but I knew my potatoes hadn't been poisoned. I'd eaten far more than she had, and I felt fine.

Was that jug of potatoes specifically set aside for Samantha?

"Who gave Samantha—the girl who passed out—her tub of potatoes?" I asked the volunteer who had handed me my jug and spoon.

She looked around. "I don't know. There were a lot of volunteers. But I think it was a man."

All the volunteers wore the same shirt—a bright orange one with running potatoes on the front. But there weren't any men within my line of sight wearing the shirt. Though, if someone poisoned her, they probably would have ditched the volunteer shirt as soon as they'd handed her the poisoned potatoes.

"You saw what happened, right?" Bonnie said from behind me, making me jump.

"No," I said. "Did you?"

"She was eating, and then she fell over," Bonnie said. "That's all I saw."

Tears filled her eyes. "They'll think it's me," she said. "First the attorney, now Samantha? Who had more to gain than I did from their deaths?"

And she had been preparing the potatoes before the race.

"It's okay. We'll talk to Jake and get everything figured out." I glanced around but didn't see Jake, Xander, or

James anywhere. "Maybe she won't die. Maybe she was just choking, and when they clear her airway, she'll come back."

"You think?" Bonnie asked. "If she does, I'll give her the farm. Or at least half. I don't even want it anymore. This town is cursed."

"Let's go find Jake," I said.

Jake, Xander, and James stood on the other side of the gazebo, where Xander pointed off toward the furthest part of the course.

"Jake?" I asked, coming up behind them. "Bonnie and I wanted to talk to you."

"Sure thing," Jake said.

Bonnie squared her shoulders. "I just wanted you to know I was with Katie and Nancy and all the others the entire race."

Jake nodded. "You're afraid we'll think you're guilty again?"

"I don't know why people around me keep dying," she said, her voice cracking a bit with emotion. "If it's because of that stupid farm, you can keep it. I'm getting out of this town just as fast as I can."

Bex joined the group and handed me Penelope. I snuggled into her warmth. I didn't realize until that moment I was shaking.

"Hold on," Xander held up a hand like he wanted to ask Bonnie a question, then turned his attention on me. "You have a pig?"

I sighed. "Yes, I have a pig."

"Like a pet pig?" Xander looked like he could not believe I would have a pig.

117

"Her name is Penelope," I said. "She's my best friend."

"A pig is your best friend?" Xander looked like he might laugh until he saw the I-dare-you look in my eye.

"Ellie," Jake said, interrupting our staring contest. "Can you tell me about the race? What happened?"

"These two," I said, motioning toward Xander and James. "Were right next to me. Then Xander went faster. Then I caught up and passed him."

"She's fast, this one," Xander said.

James looked irritated that Xander was praising me. Bex smiled—thrilled to watch the drama unfolding.

"When I got close to the finish, I turned to look back, and Samantha and Missy were in their own little race," I said. "I had to pick up my speed to keep them from beating me."

Nancy, Fran, Amy, and Katie came walking up next to us.

"What a race," Fran said. "Thanks for making me twenty bucks richer." She squeezed my shoulder. I tried to smile at her, but I just wasn't feeling very chipper.

"The four of you were working the potato stand before the race, right?" Jake asked Nancy, Fran, Amy, and Bonnie.

They nodded.

"I was in charge," Nancy said.

"Did you see anything, Miss Nancy?" Jake asked.

"Nothing suspicious," Nancy said. "I know those potatoes were perfectly okay. I made them myself."

Katie cleared her throat.

"Katie helped too," Nancy said.

"And then you ran the race, right?" Jake asked.

"Yep, we left the containers with the volunteers,"

Nancy said, then her already big eyes got bigger. "Do you think one of them messed with Samantha's taters?"

"One of the volunteers—the one who handed me my potatoes," I said. "She told me a man handed Samantha her jug of potatoes. Do you think you could get us a list of all the men who signed up to volunteer?"

Nancy frowned. "That's impossible," she said. "There were no men volunteering. I only got ladies this year."

I glanced at Jake, who asked, "Do you think you could track down the female volunteer you spoke with so we could ask her some more questions?"

The park was clearing out—only a few people in bright orange shirts remained.

"She's right there." I pointed to a woman by the gazebo.

Jake nodded. "I'll go talk to her. I'll be right back." The way he said it was clearly a hint that I was not invited to the conversation.

Once he was gone, Bonnie said, "I just hope Samantha's okay."

"Why?" Katie asked. "Now you have the farm all to yourself. And Helen's and the company. Seems awfully handy, if you know what I mean."

I gave Katie a look. "What did I say about being nice?"

"I wasn't bullying," Katie said. "I was just telling it like it is."

"She's right," Bonnie said. "It looks suspicious. Which is why I'm leaving. As long as Jake doesn't need me to stay in town, I'm gone. I'm going back to Chicago, where I belong."

"Now, you can't just leave," Nancy said, shooting Katie a glare. "We were just getting to know you."

I shook my head. These women would be the death of me.

"Samantha was a bit like family, you know," Bonnie said to me. "Even though we weren't on the best of terms. She was basically all I had left of PJ. I wouldn't kill her. I wouldn't kill anyone. That property is not worth all of this. It's just some stupid farm. Not that that's bad," she added quickly when she noticed the others' expressions of disgust. "I just don't need the bad juju in my life. I'm selling the farm. And the hardware store. I'll go back to developing in places where people want me."

"We want you here," I said. "We know you didn't kill them." I mean, we didn't, but I couldn't let her just stand there and take the blame.

"Of course, she didn't. You did," Beth said, appearing behind Bex and pointing a finger directly at me.

Wow, our time decorating together really didn't stick, did it? Maybe she was just frustrated that all her hard work on the benches had blown away.

"Why would Ellie kill Samantha?" Bex asked.

"I don't think she necessarily meant to," Beth said. "But don't you find it strange that both times the women died, Ellie had just won something? She was celebrating, and both women died. Maybe she did it on purpose, or maybe she just can't control her magic."

"Magic?" James asked. "What is she talking about?"

"Oh, you didn't know?" Xander asked. "Ellie's a witch."

"She's not a witch," Bex and Nancy said together.

James turned ghostly white. "But, I thought—"

Xander looked thrilled at James' reaction.

"You know what, it doesn't matter," James said. "I think I'll head out. I have some plans this afternoon and—uh—yeah." He started to back away. "And forget I said anything about a date. You can just delete my number."

Typical. That's what usually happened when someone found out about my hair. But just the mere mention of me being a witch sent him packing. Good riddance. I didn't need yet another man who couldn't appreciate me for who I was.

"Ouch," Xander said. "That must sting."

I tried to keep a neutral expression. "It's not the first time a man went running when they found out who I am."

"PJ did the same thing," Bonnie said. "I'm so sorry, sweetie."

"Wait," Xander said. "You dated her dead son?"

"I think it's time for us to go," I said, squeezing Penelope. "I'm freezing."

"But you can't go," Nancy said. "We have to crown you the Trot 'n Tater Champion."

She grabbed my arm with more strength than an older woman should have. I suppose my morning workouts were doing some good.

As the square cleared out, racers trickled in, completely unaware of what had taken place.

"Here she is," Katie said into the microphone after climbing the gazebo stairs. "Come on up here, Ellie!"

Nancy led me up the white-washed gazebo steps where the Trot 'n Tater trophy sat on a table surrounded by other medals and awards.

"Now, everyone gets a Trot 'n Tater medal for participating," Katie said into the microphone, her voice echoing through the square. "But because Ellie finished the race and ate the potatoes fastest, she is the winner of the Trot 'n Tater trophy."

Several people cheered around the gazebo.

I looked out to find Bex and Bonnie standing together, with Xander a bit behind them. As I looked further, Chad stood toward the back of the crowd, staring straight at me. And it looked like something bright orange was sticking out below his jacket.

He knew I was the one who yelled at him. Who had seen him breaking into Samantha's car. And he was wearing something orange. Like the volunteer shirts.

If someone poisoned Samantha, he was the most logical suspect.

I glanced at Katie. She was giving some sort of Trot 'n Tater speech about the history of the event. I needed to find Jake and tell him about Chad breaking into her car. And about the t-shirt. But Jake wasn't there, and when I turned back, Chad was gone too.

No, he couldn't be gone. Dangit.

Penelope let out an oink in my arms, alerting me that my hair was changing colors. "It's okay," I said. "It's covered."

She let out another little oink.

"Now, let's give Ellie another round of applause," Katie said, jerking my attention back to the award ceremony. "If anyone wants to warm up with hot cocoa or apple cider, come on over to Katie's Café. You can even meet Ellie, have her sign an autograph, and take a picture with the famous Trot 'n Tater Trophy."

I hadn't realized winning the race came with such high expectations. Thankfully, no one wanted my autograph. Not a single picture was taken. In fact, Penelope and I were out of Katie's within the hour. Xander didn't even show up.

Not that I cared.

14

When I got home, I put the Trot 'n Tater trophy on the mantle next to a picture of Penelope and me at the Four Corners during one of our adventures. While I sometimes missed going on road trips at the drop of a hat, I was so happy to have a place to call home. Mona was home in a way, but not the same kind of home as Esme's house.

I dialed Jake's number. He picked up on the first ring.

"Ellie? Is everything okay?"

"Everything's fine," I said. "Do you have a second to talk?"

"I sure do," he said.

"Today, during the race, when I passed the B&B, I saw a man trying to break into Samantha's car," I said. "It was Malen's husband—Chad. I yelled at him, and he ran."

"Interesting," he said.

"And then he was there when Katie was giving me the trophy," I said. "And it looked like he might have been wearing an orange shirt under his jacket."

"Like the ones the volunteers wore."

"Exactly," I said. "If someone poisoned Samantha, Chad might be our—your—best suspect."

"Just like you said before." Jake sighed. "I don't think I need to tell you this, but just in case, be careful. Two women have died now, and we don't know why."

"I'll be careful," I said. "What should I do with Samantha's stuff? It's all upstairs in Rainbow." I was getting choked up again.

"How about I come over and get it," he said. "I have to notify the next of kin. But before I give them her belongings, I'd like to look through them to make sure there's nothing that could be evidence."

"Okay," I said. "Thanks."

When we disconnected, an overwhelming feeling took hold of my scalp. It was almost the same as the one I'd had when I'd been at the B&B, and someone was trying to get inside Samantha and Malen's room. It wanted me to go upstairs.

Penelope followed me up the stairs. Just before I reached the top, I heard it.

A door handle. Someone was jiggling a door handle.

None of the bedrooms in my house were locked. I'd checked the night before.

I peeked up over the top of the steps to see Chad trying every handle going up and down the hallway. Had he not heard me talking on the phone? I hadn't exactly been quiet.

"Come on," he said, pulling on the handle of Borealis.

Then he turned and caught sight of me.

His anger was apparent, and my hair blazed.

I snatched up Penelope and rushed back downstairs.

"Come back," he yelled. "I won't hurt you."

I seriously doubted that. If my hair was right, this guy killed two women, tried to break into their B&B room, their car, and had broken into my house.

I ran as fast as I could toward the back door, but Chad was faster than me. If he'd have entered the Trot 'n Tater, he would have easily won.

He grabbed my arm before I could open the door. I let Penelope down and told her to run. She charged out of the house. I could only hope Jake would make it before this crazy man killed me.

"Why are you running?" he asked.

"What are you doing in my house?" I was out of breath, and his grip would easily leave a bruise on my arm.

"The same thing I was trying to do in Samantha's car," he said.

"Destroying evidence?"

"Evidence of what?"

I tried to pull my arm away, but he gripped tighter. "Let go."

"Not until you tell me what you're talking about."

That answer was not satisfactory. My hair ignited, and perhaps my skin did too because Chad yanked his hand away like he'd do if he touched a hot stove.

"What the hell was that?" He took two steps back, his eyes going to my hair.

"You killed your wife and her—"

"Lover?"

I gasped. "You knew?" That would make sense and give him an even bigger reason to kill them both.

I needed to get out of here.

Away from him.

"Of course, I knew," he said. "That's why she was leaving me. When PJ died, there was no reason for them to be apart. Never mind, Malen had a husband."

"I'm sorry for your loss. For their affair," I said. "But why are you here?"

"Samantha had something of Malen's," he said. "Something I wanted back."

"What exactly did she have?" I asked.

"Divorce papers," he said. "She had the signed divorce papers."

"They were in the B&B," I said. "That's why you were trying to break into the room the other day."

"I didn't try to break into the room at the B&B," he said. "I tried to get into the car, but not the room."

Either he was a liar, or there was another person who wanted in that room.

"Why would you care about divorce papers? It's not like they matter now."

"I didn't want word getting out that we were having marital problems," he said. "Since she was gone, I didn't think it was important for other people to know. I guess I wanted to save face. Keep my dignity intact."

"But Samantha knew," I said. "Is that why you hurt Samantha?"

"I didn't hurt either of them," he said. "I had already left the bowling alley when everything happened with

Malen. I was down the street at a bar. You can call the bartender and ask."

"You can tell that to the police," I said. "When they get here."

"I already told the police." He looked around. "And I'm not stupid. The police aren't coming. You didn't have time to call them. Or are you telling me your little pig will do it for you?"

Penelope was pretty smart. I wouldn't put it past her.

"Fine, whatever you want to believe," I said. "The divorce papers aren't here. They're in the room at the B&B. I saw them." I pointed to the door. "Now, get out of my house."

"I don't have a car," he said. "And it's freezing outside."

When the sun went down, the wind had picked up, and it was easily below zero with the wind chill.

"Well, I'm not taking you . . . wherever it is you need to go."

"Can I call my car service to come back and wait here?" His posture relaxed. "I'm sorry I grabbed you. I just wanted you to know I wouldn't hurt you."

"Fine," I said. "Call your car, sit in there, and don't move until it gets here."

I knew full well Jake would be here before the hired car, and I would be pressing charges.

Chad went into the living room and sat on the same couch I'd sat on with Samantha just a couple of days before.

I walked into the kitchen and grabbed the biggest knife I could find from the butcher block on the island. If he came at me again, I'd stab him. Or at least I'd try. I didn't love the idea of hurting others.

Within five minutes, Penelope burst through the pig door, and Jake knocked behind her.

I opened the door and let him in.

"Are you okay?" he asked. "Penelope seems worried."

"Chad is here," I said. "In the living room."

"You let him in your house?" Jake asked.

I frowned. "He broke in. I found him trying to get into the rooms upstairs right after I got off the phone with you. He said he was trying to find the divorce papers, but I think there's more to the story."

Chad was passed out on the couch, curled up in a blanket when we walked into the living room.

Jake tapped Chad on the shoulder.

Instantly Chad's head popped up. "What? Where am I?"

He looked around, and his gaze rested on me.

"Oh, sorry," he said. "I didn't mean to doze off. This couch is incredibly comfortable."

I didn't reply.

Jake sat in a chair across from the sofa, Penelope sat next to Jake, and I stood next to the fireplace. The adrenaline was wearing off, and I was starting to shiver.

"Can you tell me why you're here?" Jake asked.

"I wanted to get some papers," Chad said.

"Divorce papers?" Jake asked.

"I didn't want word to get out that I was getting divorced." He paused. "While we're asking questions, can you tell me what happened to my wife?"

"We don't know yet," Jake said. "The autopsy hasn't been completed."

"So, what? You guys are just hanging out waiting for an autopsy?"

"Mr. Smith," Jake said, his tone kind but firm. "Your wife's case is not within my jurisdiction. Samantha's is, but you're not here to ask about her, right?"

"The last thing I care about is Samantha," Chad said. "I didn't do it, but I'm not one bit sad she's gone."

I did a mental head slap. Did this guy want to be arrested?

"Weren't you taking over Samantha's case?" I asked. "Why would your firm transfer Malen off of it when she liked Samantha and put you on it when you didn't? That doesn't seem to be in the client's best interest."

"If she didn't like it, she could have fired us and found new representation," Chad said. "In fact, that's what I was hoping for when I made the decision."

"You made the decision?" I asked.

"I'm a partner," Chad said, frowning. "I can make changes like that whenever I please."

It was no surprise Malen wanted to divorce this guy.

"Why were you trying to get Samantha to drop your firm?" Jake asked.

"It wasn't like I didn't want her case." Chad shrugged. "I just wanted to keep Samantha and Malen away from one another."

"Why?" Jake asked. I pretended not to know.

Chad stood and grabbed the blanket he'd been curled up in, folding it neatly. "This can't go anywhere," he said. "But Malen and Samantha were having an affair."

Jake's eyes grew about three sizes. "They were what?"

"It's why she wanted a divorce," he said, still not looking at us.

"And now they're both dead," Jake said.

"I know," Chad said, laying the blanket on the couch and smoothing it more nicely than it had been when he'd gotten there. "It looks like I did it. Trust me. I can see that. But it wasn't me. I wasn't happy about the infidelity —on either of their parts—but I hadn't been the most faithful guy in the world either."

"Wait, so you were cheating on her too?" I asked.

"Here and there," he said. "Nothing serious like her, though."

"Can you please take off your jacket?" I asked.

"Why?" Chad said, his face reddening slightly. "I'm freezing. Do you even have a heater in this house?"

Even though I was still shaking, the house wasn't cold.

"Please take off your jacket," Jake said. "If you want to prove your innocence, you'll take it off."

"How does taking off my jacket prove my innocence?" Chad asked, folding his arms over his chest.

"When you were in the crowd, I noticed an orange shirt peeking out from beneath your jacket," I said. "Just like the ones the volunteers wore. If you pretended to be a volunteer, you could have easily slipped something in Samantha's potatoes."

He looked at me like I was speaking in a different language. "You think I posed as a volunteer? How would that have worked?" He unzipped his jacket. "I was just at the B&B. You saw me. How would I have gotten to the square so quickly?"

"You can definitely run."

Under the jacket, a peep of orange was visible, but when he pulled it off, it was simply an orange polo.

"Satisfied?" He zipped the jacket back up.

Maybe he hadn't killed Samantha after all. Or maybe he'd planned it with the orange polo.

"You know what?" he said. "I'm out of here. I'll walk if I have to."

He began to leave, but Penelope stepped in front of him.

"Get out of the way," he said. But every time he moved, she did too.

"Penelope, let him leave," I said.

She didn't look at me.

Chad turned back to look at me, furious. "Get your stupid porker out of my way."

I hurried over to Penelope to pick her up, but she wiggled so much, I thought I might drop her.

"This is ridiculous," Chad said. "I should have never come here."

"You're right about that," Jake said. "You shouldn't have." Jake looked out the window.

I followed his gaze to find Trent and Deb walking toward the house, both of their police cars in the driveway behind Jake's truck.

"What the heck?" Chad asked when he saw them.

Deb was holding a pair of handcuffs.

"You're arresting me?" Chad said. "Why?"

"We can talk about that down at the station," Jake said. "But first and foremost, for breaking and entering."

Jake smiled at me.

Chad didn't seem to like that answer. He bolted toward the back door.

Penelope took off after him.

She might not have been as fast as me running, but she was no slouch. She caught up with him as he was trying to unlock the sticky deadbolt.

He glanced down as she weaved between his feet. It looked like he might step on her before his legs collapsed beneath him, and he crumpled to the floor.

Penelope sat just out of his reach.

Deb walked in, looked around, and hurried to cuff Chad.

"Did you find what you were looking for?" Jake asked Trent.

"It was there," Trent said, holding up an orange t-shirt in a plastic bag. "Right next to the bed."

"That was where?" Chad asked. "What does that have to do with me."

"Give it a rest," Trent said. "We know you killed Samantha and Malen. You acted like a volunteer and gave Samantha a tainted tub of potatoes."

"I didn't," Chad said. "I wouldn't." He looked at the plastic bag. "You found that on my floor? At the B&B?"

Trent didn't answer.

"I'm not proud of this, but I hooked up with one of the volunteers. She must have left her t-shirt," Chad said.

I couldn't tell if he was telling the truth or not. It seemed possible, except for the fact that the volunteer I'd talked to said she saw a man in an orange shirt hand Samantha her tub of potatoes.

"Don't you think Samantha would have recognized me

when I handed her the potatoes?" Chad said. "She never would have taken them from me. She hated me."

"We'll discuss this at the station," Jake said, then looked at Deb. "Go ahead."

She led Chad out my front door. We followed.

"I didn't do this. Find the woman I hooked up with. She'll tell you."

I looked at Jake.

"What was her name?" Jake asked.

"Brooke?" he said. "Hannah? I don't know. She was blonde."

Deb looked like she wanted to shove him down the porch steps.

"Save your breath," Trent said. "You have the right to remain silent."

He went through the rest of Chad's rights while Jake, Penelope, and I stood inside.

"Any feelings about the case?" Jake asked.

I wanted to yell at him for relying on my feelings so much. Didn't he know I had no control over them? How unreliable they were? Plus, Trent said he'd gotten in trouble for using Esme's feelings. "I don't know," I finally said.

"Well, if it's not him, it's probably Bonnie," Jake said.

"It wasn't Bonnie." This I knew. Not a feeling, but a . . . feeling. Ugh.

"I know you've formed a neighborly relationship, but money motivates a lot of things. Not only would a court case like that cost a fortune, if she lost the farm, she'd lose a bunch of future income."

"But she knew she couldn't develop," I said. "Malen

told her that right before Malen died. And she seemed pretty sad about Samantha's death. Plus, it sounds like she might sell just to get the heck out of here."

"I don't blame her," Jake said. "There's been a lot of death and destruction around since she's arrived."

Or since I'd arrived, I thought to myself.

15

I tucked Penelope into bed and headed out. I needed something to clear my mind, and I thought a beer and a game of pool might do it. What did it matter if I went to the bar Chad claimed he'd been at when Malen died?

I threw on a pair of jeans with holes in the knees and a cute sweater, tying my hair back into a loose ponytail.

Mona seemed only too happy to start up and head out into the cold. Sometimes she wasn't so easily persuaded.

When I walked into the small bar a few doors down from the bowling alley, no one looked up. No one seemed to care I was there. Which was fine by me.

I sat at the bar and ordered a beer.

"Here you go," the bartender said. "That'll be six bucks."

I handed him a ten, but before I let him take it, I said, "Have you seen someone in this bar by the name of Chad Smith?"

He let go of the money. "I don't take bribes, and I

don't comment on other customers. Unless you're the police and have a warrant."

I sighed and put the ten on the counter. "Keep the change."

Two men in their early twenties occupied the single pool table. "Can I play winner?" I asked when one of them finished their shot.

They both looked up at me. "Uh, sure," one of them said.

I sat on a stool and watched how each of them played.

When one easily beat the other, the loser handed me his stick. I chalked it up.

"Do you want to break?" my opponent asked.

"Sure," I said.

Balls scattered all over the place, kind of like my thoughts. Two of them sank into the pockets—both stripes. I sank another stripe to solidify that I was stripes, and he was solids.

Every ball I sank felt like a piece of a big puzzle. If only this case worked that way.

Chad's alibis were sketchy, and they found the shirt in his room. Even though the bartender had verified nothing, Chad could have easily come to the bar after he did something to Malen.

And if he was worried about news of the divorce getting out, he would probably be ten times more worried about people knowing that his wife was leaving him for a woman. Killing them both could have solved all of his egotistical problems.

But Bonnie also had motive. Lots of it. And her alibis weren't terribly strong either. She had been helping with the potatoes, and she was standing right next to Malen when the lights went out. It was awfully handy that she'd passed out and ended up in her driveway.

None of it made any sense. Or a lot of it made sense but didn't feel right.

I might not have had Esme's talents, but I had my gut —or scalp—feelings, and they were telling me it wasn't Bonnie and maybe not even Chad.

But if not either of them, then who?

The two cases might not have been related. Maybe Malen had a heart attack, and Samantha had choked on potatoes. Maybe this wasn't anything nefarious at all.

I sunk the eight ball and stood up to find three men gaping at me. Well, two of them were gaping. One had a grin on his face—Xander.

"Sorry," I said and handed the pool cue back to the guy who lost the last game.

He took it but said nothing.

"I think you deserve a drink for that one," Xander said.

I finished the rest of my beer and nodded. "I'm good with that." If only Beth was there to see that no one died when I won the game.

Xander ordered two beers at the bar and then turned to me. "Those guys are still looking over here."

"What, have they never seen a woman win a game of pool before?"

"You didn't just win," Xander said. "You killed it. You used your magic again, didn't you?"

I tried to determine whether my hair was acting up at all, but it didn't feel like it. "If I did, it was unintentional."

He smiled. "The first step is admitting you have powers. Congratulations."

"First step? I didn't admit anything," I said. "And how do you know? Are you a witch?"

"Men are not considered witches," he said.

"Are you the male equivalent to a witch? A wizard?"

He winced. "Stop. You sound like a children's book. A wizard? Come on." He picked up the two beers, handing me mine. "Male witches are called warlocks."

"Are you a warlock, then?"

He led me to a booth closer to the front door. "Why in the world would I tell you that?"

I sighed. "Fine, don't tell me. It's not like I even care."

He raised one eyebrow and grinned. "You don't?"

Okay, maybe I did.

"What are you doing here?" I asked, changing the subject.

"Can't a guy get a beer? Why the twenty questions?"

I was getting nowhere with this guy.

I turned and checked out the rest of the bar.

A woman who looked like she'd had five drinks too many was singing a karaoke song by Celine Dion in a key I didn't know existed. I smiled at her gumption.

At least she had the guts to get up there. It probably helped that her friends were cheering her on.

Jealousy pushed into my chest.

"Sorry," Xander said. "I wasn't trying to irritate you."

"It's not you," I said, pushing away the jealousy. I had friends. Mona and Penelope would always be there for me. Even if they couldn't exactly cheer me on.

139

But Bex would cheer me on. Or jump on stage and embarrass herself with me.

"Are you hungry?" Xander asked. "Food always makes me feel better."

"Actually, I am."

Xander waved over a waitress who practically swooned when he spoke. "Would you please get me a cheeseburger and whatever she would like?" He handed her a credit card.

"Oh, you don't have to pay for me," I said. "I'm perfectly happy paying for my own." I fished through my satchel, trying to find the wad of cash I'd thrown in before leaving the house.

"I think this woman is busy, El," Xander said. "Why don't you just give her your order, and you can get the next round?"

I stopped rifling in my satchel. It was as if my limbs had been frozen in shock. No one had ever called me anything but Ellie. Not one of my boyfriends or foster families had ever given me a nickname. And here Xander was calling me El.

"I can come back," the woman said, looking around the room.

I instantly felt bad. "I'll have some nachos, please."

"With meat or without?" she asked.

"Is it pork?"

"Beef."

"With meat, please."

She nodded and flashed another smile at Xander before heading back to the bar.

"Why did you call me El?" I asked, shoving everything back in my satchel.

"Your name's Ellie. I just shortened it," he said. "Is that a problem?"

I didn't know whether it was or not. My emotions were all jumbled.

"Look, I'm not here to hit on you," Xander said. "I came to town on business."

"What kind of business?"

He looked at me with a raised eyebrow again.

"So you're not going to answer any of my questions?"

"Not the ones about my job or being a warlock." He shrugged. "You could ask me my favorite color. Or food. Or why I prefer brunettes over blondes."

I scoffed.

He might have been nice to look at, but he had walls built inside him higher than my own.

"There it is again," he said, looking at my hair.

"What?" I reached up and grabbed a piece from the ponytail. It was darkening to brown. How embarrassing. I willed my hair back to normal. If I turned into a brunette the minute he brought up that he preferred brunettes, he'd think I was trying to impress him.

Was I?

No.

I wasn't. I just went for the bad boys.

Nothing else.

"Your magic is baffling," he said. "I've never seen anything like it."

"Then I suppose you never met my mother or grand-mother," I said. "Their magic was similar to mine."

"Was?"

"Well, my grandmother is no longer with us," I said. "That's the reason I'm here. She left me her farm."

"And your mother?"

I shrugged. "I have no idea. She dropped me off at a fire station when I was a baby. No one knew she was even pregnant, and no one has seen her since."

"Is that so?" He didn't look convinced of my story. "Are you angry she did that?"

"I mean, angry?" I considered this a moment. "No, not angry," I finally said. "Hurt and confused, yes. But definitely not angry."

"Really?" he asked. "Because I would be."

I shrugged. "I guess I'd like to think she had a good reason. That if she could be with me, she would."

He quirked an eyebrow up as if he didn't believe me.

But before I could react to his skepticism, the waitress was dropping off our food.

I ate like I hadn't eaten all day.

"Wow," Xander said when I finished the entire plate of yummy chips, cheese, beef, and veggies. "I'm impressed."

"With what?"

"You should enter more eating contests."

I dabbed at the corners of my mouth with the little square napkin that had been under my beer. "What can I say? I like to eat." I shrugged.

He laughed. It was the first time I'd seen him genuinely smile, and it almost knocked me over. It was a good thing I was sitting in a booth.

"Now that you're done, why don't you tell me about this case you're working on?" Xander said, picking at his fries. It seemed he only liked the ones with pointy ends, leaving all the perfectly good ones with square ends uneaten.

"I don't know that I should talk about it," I said. "And honestly, it's not my case. It's the police's case."

"Then why are you looking into it?" he asked. "Isn't that why you came here tonight? You were hoping to find that girl's husband?"

"What girl's husband?" I asked.

"The one who died at the bowling alley."

"Why would I come here to find him?" I was thoroughly confused. "He's in jail."

"He is?" Xander motioned toward the door where Chad stood, surrounded by Missy, Janelle, and Becky.

"The police arrested him at my house today," I said. "How did he get out so fast?"

"Maybe his alibis checked out?" Xander said. "Or he lawyered up."

That was probably it. He was probably out on bail.

"You know, he's been in this bar every night for the past week, but he's never been here with three girls. His max before now was two."

I felt the sudden urge to give Chad a piece of my mind. How dare he act so horrible when his wife had just died?

"How do you know he's been in the bar every night? Do you come to the bar every night too?"

Xander shrugged but didn't answer my question.

"That guy is a total player," Xander said. "He's either come or gone with a woman every time he's been here."

"What about the night of the murder?" I asked. "Were you here that night?"

"I think he was with a blonde," he said. "But it all runs together when there are so many."

Anger threatened to burst from my scalp. My hair would be bright red if I didn't simmer down a bit. I took a deep breath. "I hate guys like that."

"Me too," Xander said, surprising me.

"You do?"

"I mean, I admire his ability to attract women," Xander said. "But I hate liars. I can't tolerate them."

"Noted," I said. "Does that mean you always tell the truth?"

He finished the rest of his beer and looked at me. "Even if it hurts."

The waitress came back and asked if he wanted another beer.

"Why don't you get me your favorite?" he said. "Ellie, you want anything?"

"I'll take the same," I said. "And I'll get it this time."

Xander shrugged and let the waitress take my debit card.

"Oh, and I have a quick question," he said, giving her his most dazzling smile.

"Sure." She tucked a piece of her hair behind her ear and leaned closer to him.

"See that man over there with the three women?" he asked.

"Yeah," she said. "He's a regular. Or at least he has been for the last week or so."

"Do you remember around what time he got here Friday night?"

"It was a bit later than usual," she said. "You were here too if I recall."

"I was," Xander said. "You have a great memory."

She smiled, obviously not caring that she was so busy anymore. Or that Xander was sitting with another woman.

"Do you remember hearing him say anything that night? I know that's a lot, so if you don't, it's okay."

"He told his date—she was blonde, I think."

Xander nodded.

"He told her that all his problems would soon be solved."

Xander glanced at me as if he'd come across some huge bit of information. But really, he could have just been talking about the divorce and kicking Malen off the case.

"Anything else?" Xander asked, grabbing her hand in his.

"That night, the woman he was with seemed different. Like she'd known him longer than the other women he'd brought in before. He held her hand and kissed her on the lips, whereas he didn't do that with anyone else."

"You have been so helpful," Xander said, bringing her hand to his mouth and kissing it gently.

She blushed. "I'll be right back with your beer."

"She's pretty," I said.

"We'll see," Xander said. "But that was good information, right?"

"Kissing someone on the lips means nothing for a cheating jerk." I shook my head. "This was a total waste of time. If anything, it just solidified what I'd already known."

"Which was?" Xander asked.

"Chad and Malen were getting divorced. He'd kicked her off Samantha's case. That's probably what he was talking about when he said his problems would be solved. He's a lawyer. I doubt he'd come into a crowded bar and admit he'd just offed his wife a few doors down."

"Good point," Xander said.

The waitress dropped off the beer and a slip to sign. I almost passed out when I saw how expensive the beer was. I'd never paid over fourteen dollars for a beer, and that was at a sporting event one of my boyfriends dragged me to. This was more than triple that. I added a tip and signed, swallowing hard.

She didn't even acknowledge me but smiled at Xander again before she walked away.

"This beer better be amazing," I said. "Careful with that one. She has expensive taste."

He and I both took a sip, and it took everything in me not to spit it out. "This is the worst beer I've ever tasted. How could she like that?"

"She doesn't," Xander said, pushing his away. "And now I know."

"Know what?"

"Whether I want to date her."

"How?"

"She lied," he said. "She promised to bring us her favorite beer, but instead, she brought us the most expensive beer so she could make a bigger tip."

"Makes sense," I said. "What doesn't make sense is this case."

"Do you even know how they died?" he asked.

"No," I said. "And there weren't any indicators of death that I could see. No blood, no injection wounds, nothing."

"Then why do you think someone murdered them?"

"It's just a feeling." I looked down at the disgusting beer I'd just paid more for than my entire grocery budget.

"Hmmm." He thought for a moment. "What's the next logical step in the investigation?"

"I'm not sure," I said. "I talked to Bonnie—she actually asked me to help find who did this. I talked to Chad. He went to jail and then got out. I was there when both women died."

"So why don't you revisit the places they died? Maybe the police missed something."

"That would be fine and dandy, but I'm pretty sure James won't want me in his bowling alley again."

"Let me handle James," Xander said, picking up his cell phone. "Yeah, hey James, it's Xander." He paused, then laughed. "You too, buddy."

Buddy? They'd become friends?

"Hey, I was wondering if Ellie and I could come by the alley and look at something tonight."

I was on the edge of my seat. I didn't know what we would find, but any small thing could make a big difference.

"Great, thanks," he said. "See you soon." He hung up and shrugged. "That wasn't so hard."

I looked down at my beer. I felt like I needed to finish it. I'd paid so much for it.

"I'll pay you for the beer." Xander pulled out a wad of cash. "Neither of us should have to drink that." He handed me the money. "Just take it."

"But you bought my nachos too."

"Getting to see you devour them as if no one was watching was well worth the price." He stood and offered a hand to help me up.

I hesitated before I took it. Would there be another spark?

"Independent woman." He pulled it back. "Sorry."

I wanted to tell him not to be sorry, but I also knew it was bad news encouraging him to flirt with me.

I took one last look at Chad, who seemed thrilled to be the center of attention before I pushed open the door. Even being drunk, I couldn't believe they were actually partying after two of their friends had died. It was the definition of tacky.

16

W hen I walked outside, the icy wind hit me square in the face. I felt like I had instant frostbite.

"Did you bring a jacket?" Xander looked at my holy jeans, his eyebrows raised.

I shook my head, wrapping my arms around myself.

"This is Iowa not Colorado. You can't just go out without a jacket. Come on." He led me to a black Harley Davidson and opened the small compartment on the back. "Here." He held a jacket out for me. "I want it back, though."

The minute I put it on, I knew there was something special about it.

"Is there magic in this jacket?" I asked, almost laughing at the thought.

"Of course, there is," he said. "Why else would it be that warm?"

He handed me a helmet.

"What exactly do you want me to do with this?"

He looked at me as if I was joking. "Put it on your head."

He put his own helmet on and threw a leg over the motorcycle. "Come on. We don't have all night."

Seeing him on a motorcycle brought back the memory of Esme's journal. "Did you ever meet my grandmother?"

He looked taken aback by my question. "Why would you ask that?"

"It's just something she wrote about—meeting a man on a motorcycle."

"I'm not the only man who owns a motorcycle." Xander smiled. "You coming?"

"I can drive myself." I handed him the helmet back. "I'll meet you there."

I hurried to Mona before he tried to change my mind.

It took a bit of sweet-talking, but she finally rumbled to life.

"I know it's cold, sweetie," I said. "But I appreciate you keeping me warm and off the back of a motorcycle."

Mona didn't respond, but that didn't keep me from talking to her.

"Xander seems nice, but in a dangerous way. Another bad boy. But at least he's an honest bad boy." I smiled. "And he let me borrow his magic jacket."

The bowling alley parking lot was empty besides Xander's motorcycle and Mona. The light-up open sign was dark, but the door was open, and James stood waiting, a tired expression on his face.

"Ooh, there he is." Xander batted his eyelashes as if he were impersonating me.

I glared at him.

"Come on. You thought he was cute. I could tell. Your magic gave you away."

"What do you mean my magic gave me away?" I whispered, hoping James couldn't hear our conversation.

"It's hard to explain," he said. "It's a mixture of the senses. I can sense your feelings the more of my senses I use."

I blushed at the thought of him using all of his senses on me. Then shook the thought away. Going for bad boys was a bad idea.

"Anyway," I said, changing the subject. "It doesn't matter what I thought. He freaked when he heard the slightest mention of magic. Look at how he's looking at me now. Like I might blast his head off or something."

Xander laughed. "Blast his head off."

I sighed. "Do women freak out when they find out you're a warlock?"

Xander looked at me. "Who says I tell them?" He turned and shook James' hand. "Thanks for letting us come in."

"Sure thing," James said, not meeting my eye. "The police just cleared the scene this afternoon. I can open back up tomorrow."

"That was quick," Xander said.

"There wasn't much evidence," James said.

When Xander turned back toward me, his face was twisted in what looked like confusion.

"What?" I put a hand up to my hair, but it felt normal. So normal, it was almost abnormal.

But Xander's gaze wasn't on my hair specifically. Trust me. I knew when someone was looking at my hair. Most women could pick out when a man looked at their cleavage—even the smallest glance. I didn't have much in that area, but I could see the same when someone looked at my hair. They'd been doing it my entire life.

"You just—" he stopped and glanced at James. "Nothing. Let's go see what we can find."

We stepped inside a dark cavern.

James flipped on the lights. "I'll be in the office if you need me."

He didn't even glance my way before he left Xander and me standing there.

"Where did it happen?" Xander asked.

I led him back to the arcade area. "Her body was here."

Xander stuck his hands in the pockets of his jeans and stared at the spot.

"What?"

"It's just weird someone died here, that's all."

It was weird, but for some reason, all I could think about was looking under the big rig machine. Probably to see if the police had found the syringe.

I got down on my hands and knees and looked, but the syringe was gone.

Good.

That meant the police had it.

But my hair tingled—telling me to keep looking.

I didn't want to reach under the machine. There could have been spiders under there.

I pulled out my cell phone and fumbled to turn on the flashlight before shining it underneath.

Nothing. Not a single thing was beneath the machine.

I turned the phone flash off and stuck it back in my satchel.

"Do you see anything?" Xander asked, still standing with his hands in his pockets.

"Not yet," I said. There was something there. I could feel it.

I glanced around the floor and then looked behind the big rig machine.

Bingo.

I reached back and retrieved a dark piece of velvet fabric—the only thing behind the machine that wasn't covered in about an inch of dust.

"What is that?"

"It's a headband," I said. "A very specific headband."

I pictured Samantha and all her friends in matching shirts and headbands.

"What? Is that important?"

I hesitated to tell him, but he *was* helping me. "This headband was part of a matching group. Malen and Samantha's team wore them as part of their uniform that night."

"It probably fell off when she died," Xander said.

I thought back to that night. "It wasn't Malen's headband. Hers was on her head."

"Maybe you just thought it was," Xander said.

"I was giving her CPR," I said. "I watched her headband bob with every chest compression."

"One of the other women?"

"If there was a struggle, one of their headbands could have fallen behind the machine."

153

My mind went back to Bonnie's disheveled appearance when she appeared on my porch early the next morning.

The only two people standing in that corner when the lights went out were Bonnie and Malen. Malen was the only one wearing a headband and still had the headband on when she was lying on the floor.

I inspected the headband a little more closely. A hair was wrapped tightly around the elastic area, almost too small to be seen. I carefully pulled the hair away and held it up to the light.

"A blonde, then?" Xander asked.

"There were two blondes in the group—Missy and Becky."

"Can you remember if either of them was missing a headband after you found the body?"

I wracked my brain, but it just wasn't coming to me. I knew Samantha had hers. She was wearing it the morning she came to demand my help.

"Hold on," I said, walking away from the arcade area and into the bathroom.

Xander followed.

"Whoa, this is the women's restroom."

"There aren't any women here," he said.

I put my hands on my hips and raised my eyebrows.

"Well, except you," he said. "Were you coming in here to use the bathroom?"

Part of me wanted to say yes. To keep him on his toes. But instead, I shook my head. "I wanted to see if any other headbands had been left," I said. "This is where Samantha and her friends were when the lights went out."

I searched the stalls but found nothing. It was as if the

bathroom had been cleaned. And it probably had been after the scene was cleared. James would have wanted a clean bathroom if he was opening the next day.

"Knock, knock?" James said from the restroom doorway.

Xander and I both emerged from the oversized accessible stall.

"Oh, wow," James said. "Sorry, dude. I didn't know."

"Ewww," I said. "In a bathroom? No." I smiled. "You didn't walk in on anything, promise."

James smiled at me, then probably remembered he was afraid of me and looked away.

"We were looking for clues," Xander said.

"In the bathroom?" James asked. "But the murder was by the arcade."

"I thought maybe I'd find something in here." I thought for a minute.

I knew Bonnie hadn't killed Malen, and I was pretty certain Chad hadn't either. But the headband behind the big rig machine told a much larger story—maybe one of the bridesmaids killed Malen.

My phone rang inside my satchel. I pulled it out to find Jake's name on the screen.

"Hello?"

James and Xander both listened.

"Bonnie turned herself in." His voice was sleepy.

"What?" I frowned. "That's impossible. Bonnie didn't kill anyone."

"I don't know whether she did or not," Jake said. "But she won't talk to Deb or me. She says she'll only talk to you. Do you think you could come down to the station tonight? I know it's late, but I'd hate to give her any more time to think. I don't want her to change her mind about talking to someone."

"I can be there in an hour," I said. "I'm up at the bowling alley with Xander. I think we found some evidence that will absolutely not implicate Bonnie."

"What kind of evidence?" Jake asked.

"A headband like the ones Samantha and Malen's bowling team wore. It was behind the big rig machine."

"And Malen was wearing hers, right?" Jake asked. He must have seen the crime scene photos.

"Yes," I said. "And so was Samantha."

"That's good to know," he said. "Do you want me to pass the information along to Trent?"

"That's up to you," I said. "I probably shouldn't have touched it, but I wasn't sure it was a piece of evidence until I was holding it."

Jake didn't respond. Was he angry that I'd messed up the case? "If you can, find a plastic bag, put it inside, and bring it with you. I'll get it to Trent."

"Thanks," I said, feeling bad that I'd made the mistake. Plus, the hair that was on it was no longer wrapped neatly around it. I'd probably dropped it on the floor somewhere.

"And Ellie," he said. "I don't really want to know, but I have to ask. Did you break into the bowling alley?"

"No," I said. "James let us in after Xander talked to him. He's here now if you need to talk to him?"

"That's okay," he said. "I believe you. I'll see you when you get here."

I hung up and looked at Xander. "Things just got complicated."

17

X ander and I thanked James and headed out.

"You don't have to come to the police station," I said. "I didn't mean to ruin your night."

Xander shrugged. "I had nothing better to do."

"Well, thanks for your help," I said, getting into Mona's driver's seat.

"It was fun," Xander said. "Even if we didn't get any real answers."

He walked to his motorcycle and put on his helmet. I turned the key, but there was nothing. Mona wasn't even trying.

"Come on," I said. "I need to get to the station."

Then I panicked. It wasn't like Mona not to respond at all. I hadn't checked to see if the wires had been tampered with.

I hopped out and hurried to the back. It was even colder than before. And though Xander's jacket—which I'd forgotten to give back—kept my torso warm, my ears felt like they might fall off. I mean, why did it need to be so cold? And if it had to be cold, shouldn't there at least be snow?

I loved snow.

I shook my head. Now was not the time to be thinking about snow. I popped open the engine compartment and looked around. Nothing seemed off. Everything was in its place.

"You okay?" Xander asked, scaring me so badly I almost hit my head on the inside of the engine compartment.

"She won't start," I said. "Won't even turn over."

"Everything look okay in there?"

I nodded. "Nothing out of the ordinary."

"Maybe the starter's bad," Xander said. "You can always ride with me."

Riding with him didn't seem as dangerous now, but it still wouldn't have been my first choice. Especially in the weather.

"Let me just try one more time," I said, getting back in the driver's seat. I hugged the steering wheel and ran my thumb over the lilacs etched in the metal. "I know it's cold," I whispered. "But the sooner we get to Cliff Haven, the sooner you get to go back in the garage. That should make you want to start."

I turned the key again, hope rising in my chest.

But no.

It wouldn't turn over.

I peeked my head out the door back to Xander, who was leaning against the van holding out the extra helmet.

I locked Mona. "I'll be back for you tomorrow," I said. "Stay safe."

Her metal warmed beneath my hand as if to say she'd be fine.

I pushed the helmet on my head and swung a leg over the motorcycle as gracefully as I could.

"Hold on," Xander said.

I hesitated to wrap my arms around his waist. The last time we touched, I'd practically been electrocuted.

"Or don't, but there's not a backrest." He started the motorcycle. "And I like to go fast."

If I had to choose between being marginally electrocuted and falling off the back of a motorcycle at high speeds, I'd go with the shock.

I slipped my arms around his waist, relieved there wasn't a shock after all.

"Good choice," he yelled over the engine noise before pulling out of the parking lot and heading toward Cliff Haven.

I glanced back once more at Mona, sad that I had to leave her behind. But I had no choice. I needed to talk to Bonnie and see why she turned herself in for a crime she didn't commit.

Though the surrounding air was easily below zero and probably lower than that with the wind chill, between the magic jacket and Xander's warmth radiating toward me, I was perfectly warm on the back of his motorcycle.

In fact, when we reached the police station, I was almost sad we'd arrived.

"Thanks for the ride." I handed him the helmet and

pulled off the jacket, causing my body to go into cold spasms.

"Keep the jacket. I think you might need it."

I pulled it back on. "Are you sure?"

"For now," he said. "You sure you don't want me to come in with you?"

"No thanks."

"I can wait and take you home when you're finished."

"I'm sure Jake will give me a ride," I said. "You go enjoy what's left of your evening."

"When do you want me to pick you up tomorrow?"

I looked at him, confused. "For what?"

"To take you back to your van," he said. "I can even help put a new starter in."

"You've worked on Volkswagens before?"

"I've worked on just about everything," he said.

"Let's say nine."

"Nine it is," he said. "I'll see you tomorrow."

I walked into the police station for the second time in three days. The receptionist didn't even take my name this time. She just waved me back. "They're waiting for you in the conference room."

I tried to remember the way back to the conference room and only made a wrong turn once into a broom closet.

When I walked in, Bonnie sat with her hands folded on top of the table, a steely look on her face.

"I'm sorry I lied to you," she said before I'd even sat down.

Jake and Deb sat opposite Bonnie. Jake pulled out a chair next to him for me to sit.

"It was wrong to lie," she said. "But I knew how it looked. I have the most motive for wanting the attorney dead."

"Can you tell us what happened?" Jake asked. "From the beginning of the night?"

She ignored him and kept her attention on me.

"I already told you I went to the bowling alley to play with Katie and the group. They wouldn't let me, but I stayed and watched, anyway. I've always found bowling fascinating." She paused. "You threw the perfect game—which would be impressive if everyone didn't suspect you of being a witch." She gave me a tiny smile, and I knew she wasn't saying it as a jab. "Everyone was celebrating when Samantha's attorney approached me to talk about the case.

"Then the lights went out, and I felt someone's hands wrap around my neck," she said. "I thought it was Malen, but then another person started hitting me in the side. I struggled to get away, but they were very strong. I clawed and kicked until I remembered I had a taser in my purse."

Jake and Deb both looked up from their notepads in surprise.

"The woman choking me started to lose her grip, allowing me to breathe again. I pushed the taser up against her, and she let go, falling to the floor."

Malen hadn't looked like she'd been in a tussle. When she was on the ground dead, she looked as good as she had been standing up.

"Either way, the next thing I knew, I'd blacked out. When I woke up in my driveway, this was attached to my forehead." Bonnie pulled a sticky note out of her purse and handed it to Jake.

In beautiful flowing handwriting, it said:

Give the farm to Samantha or else.

Bonnie looked relieved to have given us her story. "Therefore, I must have killed the attorney. I probably got her with the taser, and it killed her."

"Why did you ask me to look into it if you thought you killed her?" I asked. "And why didn't you show me the note?"

"I didn't show you the note because of my pride. Imagine waking up with a threatening sticky note on your forehead." She shuttered. "And I hoped I hadn't killed Malen," Bonnie said. "I thought maybe someone else had, and you'd find them. But the most logical conclusion is that it was me."

"I didn't think tasers were lethal," I said. "Don't the police use them all the time?"

"Not all the time," Deb said, disgusted. "But sometimes. And the shock is not usually lethal unless the victim has a bad heart. Then it can cause cardiac arrest."

Jake frowned. "I'm afraid this means we have to take you into custody."

"But—" I stood, but Jake shot me a look that told me not to interfere.

Deb cuffed and read Bonnie her rights before leading her out of the room.

Bonnie went willingly, looking defeated.

"What about Chad?" I asked Jake when Bonnie and Deb were gone.

"The woman he was with came forward," he said. "She and her friends solidified his alibi. He was with her before the race and left her shirt in his room."

"What about after? Maybe he'd worn her shirt and handed out the potatoes to Samantha."

"The shirt was extra small. Chad is at least a large, if not extra-large," Jake said. "Her shirt wouldn't have fit him."

I couldn't believe they'd just let Chad off the hook so easily.

"Did Malen even die of a heart attack?" I asked.

"The preliminary report indicates a heart attack, yes," Jake said.

I gaped at him. "But she acted in self-defense," I said. "She was trying to stay alive."

"That's for a jury to decide," he said. "I can only go by the facts. If you attack someone and they die, even if you don't mean to kill them, there are still repercussions."

I was so angry I could spit.

"I think we need to talk to Samantha and Malen's friends," I said. "They'll know a little more about what happened that night. Especially since I found this behind the big rig game." I pulled out the bag James had given me with the headband inside. "I thought maybe they killed Malen, but if Bonnie's taser killed Malen only because the others attacked her, shouldn't they be brought up on murder charges too? At least second or third-degree or something?"

Jake thought for a moment. "If Bonnie killed Malen

because it was dark and she was fighting for her life from someone else, then the jury would likely let her off the hook."

"But you still won't let her go? Even though she didn't mean to do it?"

Jake shook his head. "I'm sorry."

I let out a grunt in frustration. "What about Samantha? Do you think Bonnie killed her too?"

"We haven't gotten any reports back on Samantha, but it seems unlikely Bonnie is the culprit in that case unless she poisoned the potatoes."

This conversation was getting us nowhere, and I was getting more and more frustrated as time went on.

"I'm going to head home," I said. "Let me know if you need me to get anyone else to confess to a crime they shouldn't be held responsible for."

Jake just stared at me. I was acting like a child, but I was mad, and I'm sure my hair was giving off all sorts of mad vibes.

"Have a good night, Ellie," he said finally.

I turned and walked out.

18

When I got outside, I remembered I had planned on asking Jake for a ride home.

Dangit.

I'd just have to run home. It was a good thing I wore sneakers and had Xander's jacket. I started off toward my house, using my anger to fuel my legs when I heard a rumbling behind me.

Xander pulled up and said over the noise of the motorcycle, "Need a ride?"

He'd waited for me?

I smiled. "Yes," I said. "But I need to go back to the bar."

I put on the helmet and got back on the back of the bike.

"It was that bad, huh?"

"Let's just say I need to figure some things out." I could only hope that Chad, Becky, Missy, and Janelle hadn't left already.

Xander took off. I wrapped my arms around his waist

and leaned my face into his back to keep my cheeks and nose warm.

"Why did you wait for me?" I yelled over the engine noise.

"I had a hunch you'd need a ride," Xander said.

"Are you a psychic warlock?" I joked.

"Not nearly as psychic as I'd like to be."

I wanted to ask a follow-up question, but he hit the throttle, and the engine roared too loudly to have a conversation.

When we got to the bar, Chad and the women were still sitting where we'd left them.

"Ellie," Janelle said when she saw me. "What are you doing here?"

She was obviously drunk, wearing a tiara and a sash that said Bride to Be. There were no matching t-shirts, no matching water bottles, no matching headbands. At least they'd given up on those things after their friends died.

"I need to talk to you," I said. "All of you. But not you." I pointed to Chad. "You stay here."

"Are you accusing them of murder too?" Chad asked. "That didn't get you very far with me."

I glared at him, grabbed Janelle's hand, and led her and the other two to a booth that was furthest from all the karaoke noise.

"What's this all about?" Missy said. She didn't seem nearly as intoxicated as the other two, who were leaning over onto each other, giggling.

"This is about one or more of you attacking Bonnie the night of Malen's death," I said.

All three of them stopped what they were doing and gaped at me.

Janelle looked at Missy, then Becky, then me. "We did nothing to Bonnie."

"We were in the bathroom when Bonnie killed Malen," Missy said.

"Bonnie might have tasered Malen, which could have caused her to go into cardiac arrest," I said. "But she only tasered her out of self-defense. And I'm guessing one of you was her attacker. Maybe two of you. And heck, maybe Malen was in on it too."

Janelle gasped. Becky rubbed her shoulder and stared at the ground. Missy looked like she might come across the table and strangle me.

"I know it likely wasn't you." I pointed to Janelle. "Because I saw you come out of the bathroom with Samantha when the lights came back on. But the two of you—now that I think about it—I didn't see either of you after the lights went out."

"I won't sit here and let you accuse us of attacking someone." Missy stood. "We did nothing wrong. We were in the bathroom the entire time."

Janelle looked at Missy as if she wanted to say something but stopped herself. She knew they weren't in the bathroom. But had she also known their plan to attack Bonnie?

If so, she could be an accessory to the murder, or at least the attack.

"Then how did one of your fancy headbands get behind the big rig machine?" I asked.

This got their attention again.

"Who's missing one?" I asked.

No one spoke. Even intoxicated, they wouldn't rat one another out. It was impressive.

"It's okay, the police will test the strand of hair that was around the headband for DNA, and they'll figure it out, eventually."

It was a tiny lie, but maybe it'd get them to talk.

"This is ridiculous," Missy said. "Let's go back to the bar."

Becky stood and followed.

Janelle hesitated but eventually followed too. She looked like she might burst into tears at any moment. I would be upset, too, if my bachelorette party week had gone the way hers had. Two friends dead. Two others committing crimes.

"Is there something else you wanted to tell me?" I asked.

She hesitated. "It's just—"

"Janelle, let's go," Missy yelled back at her.

That woman was really getting on my nerves.

"Sorry," Janelle said. "I have to go." She rejoined her friends at the bar.

Xander and Chad were having a random conversation about football when I got back. The girls stood on the other side of Chad as if they needed protection from me.

"Did they confess?" Xander asked when I came to stand next to him.

"Who confess what?" Chad asked. "They didn't kill anyone."

"They may not have killed Malen themselves, but they attacked Bonnie. Gave her a warning. But she tried to protect herself and, in the process, may have caused your wife's death," I said matter-of-factly.

Both Xander and Chad gaped at me.

"We did not, and if you continue to say those things, I'll sue you for slander," Missy said. "Chad will represent me." She grabbed his arm.

"Is any of this true?" he asked, covering her hand with his.

"Absolutely, not," Missy said. "She's just trying to protect her precious neighbor. She never liked Samantha because PJ chose Samantha over her."

I shook my head. "What are you talking about?"

"PJ never wanted to marry you. He wanted to marry Samantha. That burns you, doesn't it?" Missy said. "Maybe if you weren't such a goody-goody, guys would actually like you."

I'd never considered myself a goody-goody, but I guess it sort of fit. "I found PJ cheating on me—not with Samantha—but with someone else. And I hate cheaters." I directed the last part at Chad.

"I think it's time we leave." Xander pulled me away by my arm sending warm sparks through my body. "It's okay. They'll get theirs. The truth will come out."

None of them looked even remotely afraid of the truth coming out. Which somehow made me even angrier. If my hair had fogged up the bathroom mirror before, I was surprised it wasn't setting off the smoke alarms now.

When we were back in the fresh air, I asked Xander if he could take me back to Mona. I wanted to give it another go since we were already there.

I unlocked the door and whispered, "Please start."

The key turned easily in the ignition, and Mona roared to life. I squeezed the steering wheel. "Good girl. Thank you."

"I guess it wasn't a starter," I said.

Xander's eyes were huge.

"What?" I asked.

He looked away. "Nothing. I'm glad you got it started."

"Thanks for the ride," I said. "I owe you one."

"That's what friends are for," he said before starting his motorcycle and tearing off in the direction opposite of Cliff Haven.

I sat there for a moment contemplating everything. Janelle wanted to tell me something but didn't. Missy acted incredibly defensive. Chad seemed genuinely angry that one of the women could have hurt Malen.

And had I just been friend-zoned?

19

My eyelids were heavy when I pulled into the garage. The sun was rising in the sky. I'd been awake more than twenty-four hours. No wonder I was tired.

I fell into bed and slept for twelve straight hours.

I'd taken Penelope to her downstairs bed before I went to bed upstairs. She didn't like it, but I knew there was a solid chance I'd sleep longer than usual, and she'd need to go out.

When I got downstairs, she greeted me with excitement. I picked her up and gave her a big hug. "Thank you for always being there for me."

She nuzzled me with her nose.

"How about we get some dinner, then work on the barn for a while?"

Penelope seemed to like that idea as she practically jumped out of my arms. I always left piggy food out for her, but she much preferred people food. Her favorite being popcorn with peanut butter.

I popped each of us a bag, and we ate popcorn, peanut butter, and a salad.

"To the barn?" I asked when we were sufficiently fed.

Penelope darted out the piggy door, and I chased after her.

I'd put up some makeshift lights so I could see when I worked in there at night. I hadn't done nearly enough, and soon it would be too cold to work outside if I didn't get the place insulated and heated.

The mural in the back was different than I'd ever seen. There were more people than expected. I'd only ever seen three at the most—the grandmother, the daughter, and the granddaughter. Of course, I equated them to Esme, Emily, and me. But this time, besides the three women, twenty or more people stood with their backs to me looking at the barn.

I'd tried to interpret the murals time after time but had been unsuccessful as of yet. None of it ever made sense.

Emily's signature graced every single one. It never faded, never changed. Sometimes I'd run my finger over the letters and imagine her painting them.

"How's it going in here?" Earl's voice came from the front of the barn.

When I turned, I had to do a double-take. The entire town—or what seemed like the entire town—was standing just beyond the large barn doors, holding tools, ladders, and portable heaters.

I turned back to look at the mural. For the first time, it seemed to have interpreted something. Except Esme and

Emily weren't among the people outside my barn. Not that I expected them to be.

"Maybe a better question would be, how can we help?" Katie added, noticing my shock.

I took a few steps toward the front of the barn. Even Deb and Jake were there. Beth and Belinda, too.

"Why are you—"

"This is what we do," Katie said, coming up beside me and wrapping an arm around my shoulder. "We help each other. We don't always have to like each other." She looked at Beth and Belinda. "But we help each other, nonetheless."

"And we hear you need to get this barn fixed up so you can open your studio." Hank—the rock 'n roll Santa and Nancy's husband—said. "You've helped almost all of us with our ailments. Soon, you'll be able to help others too."

I wiped the tears from my eye and ran a hand through my hair as Penelope oinked, letting me know it had changed. "Well then," I said. "Let's get started."

We started work with the basics—sweeping and throwing away the trash. If anyone noticed the mural at the back of the barn, no one said a word. Maybe they were too busy working. Or maybe they couldn't see it. Either way, I was thankful not to have to explain it. Not that I would have been able to.

A couple of farmers brought tractors to pull my old one out and put it under a tarp behind the barn. I assured them I still wanted it, and that I would try to get it running. They laughed but humored me.

Around daybreak, Katie and Nancy headed into the kitchen to make breakfast. When they came back in with piping hot plates of eggs, toast, biscuits, sausage, and coffee, we all took a break to enjoy.

The barn was clean. We'd ripped out all the boards from the floor that seemed to have been permanently stained with manure, gotten rid of the cobwebs, taken out everything that didn't belong, and painted all but one of the walls—the one with the mural.

"Your mother was a very talented artist." Fran stood next to me as I devoured a plate of eggs and toast. She was looking at the mural just behind me. "She used to do the sets for Katie's plays." She paused. "I wonder why she didn't add any people?"

I glanced back at the wall—there were people. Lots of people. But I didn't want to contradict her. It might make me seem crazy.

"Why would that be strange?" I asked, fishing for more information.

"She always added people," Fran said. "Whether it was her and Esme, or people she didn't know, there were always people in her work."

"Maybe she ran out of time," I said with a shrug.

Fran looked at me with significance. "Maybe she did."

After everyone had eaten, they left Penelope and me standing in the big open barn all by ourselves.

As tired as I was, my heart was full.

"Oh, Penelope, can you imagine? Having my studio here?" I could see it when I closed my eyes. "I'll put mirrors up on that wall, a glossy hardwood floor

174

throughout the front half, and a sturdier carpet for the back. And I'll hang beautiful lights to create a fun, happy ambiance." I squeezed her a bit. "It'll be perfect."

Penelope oinked in agreement.

When I closed up the barn later that afternoon and glanced over to see Bonnie's house, my mood dampened a bit. Her house was dark. Completely dark.

It wasn't fair that she'd been put in jail when there was probably evidence in that very house that implicated Missy and Becky in her attack. But even if she was my neighbor, breaking in was still a crime.

It was frustrating, but not frustrating enough to keep me from falling into a deep sleep.

When I woke up, the early morning sun was shining on my face.

Then an image from my dream came back to me—Bonnie watering the plants the other morning. I needed to water her plants for her. But first, I needed her permission.

I drove to the police station and asked if I could visit one of the inmates.

I was in luck because the receptionist led me into a visiting room divided by plexiglass with a phone on each side.

Bonnie walked in, looking as put together as one could in an orange jumpsuit.

"Hello," she said when she picked up the phone.

"How are you?" I asked.

"You'd think they'd put me in solitary or make my life miserable after killing someone, but they treat me okay."

"I still don't think you killed her," I said. "And even if you did, it was out of self-defense."

"Either way," Bonnie said. "Being responsible for someone's death is not a great feeling."

I couldn't imagine it was. "What about Samantha? You didn't kill her too, did you?" I laughed at my stupid joke. We both knew she was nowhere near Samantha when she died.

"I don't know what happened to Samantha," Bonnie said. "I have no way of taking responsibility for that one."

I thought for a minute. It just didn't line up.

"Why did you come here?" Bonnie asked. "I'm not taking back my admission of guilt, not that I could now if I wanted to."

"I actually came to see if you wanted me to water your flowers," I said.

Her eyes grew. "My flowers? How did you—oh—you saw me watering them in my window."

"Is that a problem?" I asked. "If so, I don't have to go over there. I just wanted to offer."

"Uh yeah," she said. "You can water them. But be careful. They're—uh—special." She looked down at her hands. "And make sure to wear the gloves."

She might not have wanted to get her hands dirty, but I didn't mind. Nonetheless, I'd use the gloves.

"Any other instructions?" I asked.

"In my bedroom, next to the bed, is a red flower. I need you to pay special attention to that one."

She said the words as if they were a matter of life and death.

"I can do that," I said.

"Thank you, Ellie," she said. "Thank you for everything. You were more than welcoming even when I was about to destroy your property value by putting in a huge development." She shook her head. "Sometimes, I can't believe myself. If I ever get out of this, I'm selling the company and moving to Aruba."

"Or you could just stay here," I said. "I hear you have a pretty fantastic neighbor."

"I hear I have two," she said. "I just haven't gotten to know one of them very well."

Katie.

She and Katie could have been great friends under different circumstances. They both liked fashion—though different types. Both were classy and kind.

"I'll come back and visit again," I said.

"Thank you for taking care of my plants," she said. "Don't forget the red one by the bed."

These plants almost sounded like her babies. Which maybe they were now that PJ was gone.

When I walked out of the visitation room, Jake stood on the opposite side of the hall, leaning against the wall. "We need to talk."

He led me back to his tiny office and asked me to take a seat.

"You know all conversations in the visitation room are recorded, right?"

I saw the sign before I walked in. But we'd only been talking about watering her flowers.

"Yes," I said. "Why?"

Jake brought the tips of his fingers together in front of his mouth like he was trying to find the best way to tell me something. "We got the autopsy results back for Samantha and an updated autopsy report for Malen."

I sat forward in my chair. "And?"

"Malen didn't die of cardiac arrest."

"Then let Bonnie go," I said, happiness flooding through me.

"They both died of poisoning," he said, ignoring my demand.

"Okay," I said, not making the connection. "What were they poisoned with?"

"Aconitum," Jake said. "Sometimes called wolfsbane."

"Like in Dracula?" I asked. "I thought that was for keeping vampires away."

Jake looked at me like I'd grown another head. "I've never seen it."

"I'm guessing whoever did this didn't think these women were vampires."

He didn't laugh.

My scalp tingled as if my hair was trying to tell me something. Like it wanted me to remember.

But what?

Wolfsbane was a plant—a flower.

And I'd just been talking to Bonnie about taking care of her flowers.

And wearing gloves.

Jake waited for the recognition to cross my face.

"You think Bonnie poisoned them?" I struggled to grasp this idea. "But then why would she have admitted to using her taser?"

"Maybe she wanted to put us off the scent. She'd be more likely to get out of trouble if she had been attacked and used her taser in self-defense."

It made sense but felt wrong. "I have permission to take care of her plants. Let's go see if she has any wolfsbane."

Jake nodded. "And I have a warrant."

Bonnie's house was spotless. And when I say spotless, I mean not a single speck of dust or dirt. The kitchen trash was empty. The dishes were in their places.

"Those are the plants." I pointed to the window where she kept them.

I hesitated. I didn't want to find out Bonnie was the one who did it. Or that she'd completely lied to me.

Jake held out his phone. "This is what the flower looks like."

I took a good look and sucked in a breath. A slight

tingle took over my scalp sending dread through me. If my scalp was tingling, it was probably telling me there was a clue here.

I put on a pair of yellow rubber gloves before examining each plant.

Some were big and some small. They were all different colors and shapes. But the weirdest thing was, their soil was damp. They didn't need to be watered. They had a self-watering drip system set up. Then why would she have told me to water them?

I pushed aside a yellow one and a leafy one before finding one that matched the color on Jake's phone—a vibrant purple.

The tingle in my scalp radiated out of my hair.

This was it.

The proof that she had, in fact, murdered two women.

Intentionally.

"I guess we have our answer," I said, letting Jake take a look.

He looked at the flower I was pointing out and then at the others. "I guess we do." He ran a hand over his head. "I was so sure."

"What do you mean?" I asked. "You were sure she was innocent?"

He shook his head. "I was sure she was guilty."

"But she is," I said. "Isn't this wolfsbane?"

Jake looked more closely at the purple flower. "This is catmint," he said. "I guess they look somewhat similar. My grandmother used to grow catmint in her garden to get rid of aphids. It's not toxic to people."

My hair felt like it was burning. "None of this makes

sense," I said. "Why would she have agreed to let me come over here to water her plants? They have a self-watering system."

"Maybe she got word that the women had been poisoned and wanted to clear her name?" Jake shook his head. "I don't know."

Then I remembered. She'd been very adamant that I water the plant in her bedroom. The red one.

"She wanted me to take care of a plant in her bedroom," I said.

"You do that, and I'll search the rest of the house."

As I approached the bedroom, my hair became almost unbearably hot. My neck dripped with sweat.

But once inside, I was at a loss. Though I could tell there was something I was meant to find, I couldn't see a single red flower. Both of her nightstands were immaculate. One simply held a book and a pair of reading glasses. The other was completely clear of anything. I peeked in the drawers, feeling slightly awkward that I was going through her personal things. But again, found nothing. Not a single red flower. Not an empty flower pot. Nothing.

Was someone setting her up? Had they taken the flower?

And why would a red flower be important unless she really had wanted me to water it?

"Did you find what you were looking for?" Jake asked when I emerged from the bedroom.

"No." I shook my head. "I'm even more confused than I was before we came. But I'm glad Bonnie's been cleared." I paused. "She has been cleared, hasn't she?"

Jake nodded. "There's no way we can hold her. Nor can Trent. When the autopsy report came back, Trent specifically asked the coroner if they saw a taser mark on Malen's body." He shook his head. "Whoever got tased wasn't Malen."

I considered this. "So Bonnie was attacked, she tased someone, then passed out."

"We think we know why Bonnie passed out too," Jake said. "That syringe you told Trent about under the arcade machine had remnants of a strong sedative inside. Something not everyone would have access to."

"Who would have access?"

"Zookeepers, doctors, veterinarians," he said. "Basically, anyone in the medical profession."

A thought popped into my head. The only person I knew with a medical background was Becky—the tiny blonde bridesmaid. "Have you spoken with Janelle's bridesmaids Becky and Missy?"

"Both Trent and I have briefly, but there's nothing we can hold them on."

Frustration rose within me. I knew Becky and Missy attacked Bonnie. I knew it. Yet, there was no evidence.

"Why don't we go get some crispy pancakes at Katie's," Jake said, glancing up at my hair.

I pulled a piece down. "Orange? Really?" I sighed. I hated orange.

Jake laughed. "When Emily was frustrated, hers turned the same color."

I wondered if ours turned the same color for all of our emotions or just some.

"Pancakes sound great," I said.

But when I tried to walk out the door, it was as if there was an invisible barrier keeping me in the house.

"Uh," I said. "I think I need to find that red flower first."

21

J ake and I searched high and low but found no red flower. We tried to leave a couple more times but, though Jake could get out, I couldn't. I'd never had my magic—or whatever—act this way. It was a bit disconcerting.

"Do you think maybe red flower was a metaphor?" Jake asked, his head in his hands as he sat on the couch. "Maybe she was trying to tell you something but knew she was being recorded."

I thought back to all the conversations I could remember having, but nothing about a red flower came up.

Then an image jumped into my mind.

I rushed back into her bedroom and to the far side of the bed. There were no flowers on the nightstand, but right next to it was a small trash can with tiny red flowers all over it. "Jake, come here."

I glanced inside to find what looked like the white shirt Bonnie had been wearing the night she was attacked.

185

"That's the shirt she was wearing the night at the bowling alley and when she came to my house the next morning."

When Jake held out the shirt, pink glitter sparkled and fluttered to the floor.

"That's it," I said. "The girls were all wearing shirts with pink glitter on them. They had to be made quickly, so they probably weren't the best quality."

"And when Missy or Becky put Bonnie into her car, the glitter would have transferred." Jake pulled out a large bag and put the shirt inside, then took pictures of the glitter on the floor. "This might be enough to at least talk to them again."

"But first, pancakes?" I asked.

"Definitely," Jake said.

The café was very quiet. The farmers weren't at their table in the back, and there wasn't a single other person dining. Bex welcomed us with a smile.

"How are the two of you this fine morning?" she asked.

"Getting better by the minute," I said. "I'll have coffee and pancakes, please."

"Make it double," Jake said.

She looked from me to Jake and back again. "Two identical orders coming up."

"What was that all about?" Jake said.

"She's convinced you're my dad," I said. "She thinks you're lying about—you know . . ." Even though he wasn't my dad, it was still awkward to talk to him about sex.

"Why would I lie about that?"

"She thinks you're lying to save face—for both you and Emily."

"Trust me," he said. "I almost wish it was possible. I'd be proud to have a daughter like you."

I could feel my scalp tingle—in a good way this time. "I wish it was possible too."

"Don't worry, kiddo," he said. "I'm not giving up hope that we'll find her. Or your dad."

"You're still looking for her?"

"Never stopped," he said. "And I probably never will."

My heart felt like it might explode. If we ever found her, I'd hug her and then give her a piece of my mind for leaving Jake and then leaving me at the fire station.

"Two plates of pancakes—crunchy bits intact," Bex said, delivering our plates. "And two coffees."

"Thanks, Bex," I said.

She slid into the chair next to me. "Have you figured anything out about the case?"

"We're working on it," I said, glancing at Jake.

"It's a toughie," he said. "Every time we think we have a lead, it's a dead end."

"Have you heard anything more about Chad or Janelle or Missy or Becky?" I asked.

"I hear tonight is the last night they'll be at the B&B. But that's about it."

"Maybe we should head over there after breakfast," I said to Jake.

"Sounds like a plan," he replied, adding a heaping

amount of syrup over his pancakes. That was one thing we didn't have in common. I didn't like my pancakes saturated with syrup.

Belinda was at the front desk when we walked in.

She was all smiles until she saw me. It was at that moment I knew our attempt to speak with the women would be met with resistance.

Even though she'd helped with the barn, it seemed to be more out of necessity than actually wanting to.

"Is there something you need?" she asked.

Jake frowned. Apparently, he wasn't used to Belinda being icy toward him.

"We'd like to speak with a couple of your guests."

"I'm sorry," Belinda said, looking at me. "If you don't have a warrant, you can't."

Jake looked back at me. Then recognition dawned on his face.

"That's fine," Jake said, turning back to Belinda. "We can just wait here for them."

"Only paying customers," Belinda said. "You understand."

"I do," Jake said, pulling a twenty-dollar bill from his pocket. "We'd like two cups of your famous coffee, please."

I'd assumed that the sitting area in the room off the foyer was for overnight guests, but then I noticed a small sign with a handful of drinks and prices next to the cash register.

Belinda took Jake's money and gave him the change. "You can just wait in there." Her voice was angry. "I'll bring them to you."

We didn't have to wait long. Simultaneously, as Belinda was dropping off our coffees, Janelle was coming down the stairs with two huge suitcases.

I jumped up. "Can I help you with those?"

Janelle smiled. "Thank you." She handed me one of the handles.

"I thought you were checking out tomorrow," I said.

"Plans changed," she said as we made our way to her car. "Missy's got a secret date planned with her secret boyfriend. And Becky picked up an early shift at the hospital tomorrow morning."

"Have they left?" I asked.

She shook her head. "They're still asleep."

I felt the cool rush of relief extinguish the anxious sensation on my scalp.

"It's probably better this way anyway," Janelle said, lifting each of the suitcases into the trunk one by one. "When two of your best friends die during your bachelorette week, it kinda puts a damper on the fun."

"You looked like you were having fun the other night at the bar," I said.

She blushed. "I was so drunk. They just kept giving me drinks, thinking it would lighten me up. I guess it did."

"There was something you wanted to tell me that night," I said. "Do you remember what it was?"

She looked down at the ground. "I probably shouldn't say anything."

"It's about what Missy and Becky did to Bonnie, isn't it?"

She nodded but still didn't look at me. "I guess Bonnie deserved it for murdering my friends, but they still shouldn't have done it."

"What were they trying to do?"

"They just wanted to scare her and make her give the farm to Samantha. We all wanted that. But they wanted to do something about it."

"So they cut the lights, injected her with something, drove her home, and left a warning note?"

She nodded again.

"Would you mind talking to the officer inside about this?"

"You'll just tell him anyway, so why not?" She threw her hands in the air. "I told them it was a bad idea."

We went back inside, and she told Jake everything she'd just told me. As she was finishing, Becky and Missy came walking into the room.

Missy looked like she might shoot fire from her eyes. "What did you just tell them?"

Janelle seemed truly scared. "I was tired of keeping the secret. You shouldn't have done it. Maybe if you hadn't, Malen and Samantha would still be here." Janelle dabbed at her eyes.

"She's lying," Missy said. "I have an alibi for that night. I was with my boyfriend."

"Oh, come off it," Becky said. "You were with me. You cut the lights. You helped me get Bonnie into her car. And you don't have a boyfriend."

Missy gasped. "I most certainly do."

"Prove it," Janelle said, standing next to Becky. "Show us a picture of the two of you together."

Missy hesitated.

"Go on," Becky said. "If you have a boyfriend, show us a picture."

Missy pulled out her phone and typed in a few things before turning the phone around.

She was kissing a man.

"This was the night Bonnie was attacked, and Malen died," she said. "It's time-stamped and everything."

Jake looked at me.

"But you were at the bowling alley," I said. "I saw you there."

"Yeah, but I left before anything happened to Malen."

"Let me see that picture," Becky said.

Missy pulled it to her chest. "No. I proved it."

"You could have kissed any guy," Janelle said. "Doesn't mean he's your boyfriend."

"And it seems awfully handy that you just happened to be kissing a guy the same night everything happened." Becky crossed her arms over her chest and looked at Missy with a challenge in her eyes.

"Okay, you don't believe me?" Missy swiped a couple of times then showed her friends the phone again. "Here."

I couldn't see the picture around Janelle's and Becky's heads, nor could I see their expressions. But their gasps were those of horror.

"Please tell me that's not who I think it is," Janelle said, grabbing the phone from Missy's hand.

Becky stepped between them as Missy reached for the phone. "Give it back."

But Janelle was facing me now, and with every swipe, her face became more and more shocked. Or maybe it was angry. I couldn't tell.

"We flirt," Becky said. "That's it."

"He loves me," Missy said. "And I love him. We're going to be together."

I stepped closer to see the phone screen.

Janelle noticed and turned it toward me. "Her boyfriend is Chad—Malen's husband."

22

That was all I needed for the pieces to click.

"How long have you been sleeping with him?" Janelle asked before I could.

"We're not just sleeping together," Missy said. "We. Are. In. Love."

"Just like he was in love with every other girl he cheated on Malen with." Becky shook her head. "Chad's trash."

"Malen ruined his self-confidence," Missy said. "How would you feel if your husband told you he was gay? After being together for so many years."

"Chad's gay?" Janelle asked.

Becky looked at Janelle as if she was joking. But Janelle seemed completely confused. Maybe she hadn't known about Malen and Samantha.

"Malen was gay," Becky said gently. "She and Samantha were in love. They had been since college."

"But—no," Janelle said. "Not that there's anything wrong with it, but I would have noticed."

"They kept it quiet," Becky said. "Until PJ died, and Malen was at Samantha's side."

"That's why they were getting a divorce?" Janelle said.

"No," Missy said. "They were getting divorced because he wanted to be with me."

"Had he signed the papers?" Becky asked, her eyes narrowing.

"No, Malen still had them." Missy snatched her phone back. "But he would have when he got them."

"Really? Because I heard him begging her to tear them up," Becky said. "I'm surprised you didn't. Your room was right next door to hers, and the walls aren't exactly soundproof."

"So that's why you did it," I said.

Missy narrowed her eyes at me. "I already told you, I had nothing to do with Bonnie's attack."

"Oh, you did," I said. "And there are two women here who can testify to that. But that's not what I was referencing."

Jake smiled. He and I must have come up with the same idea at the same time.

"Do you want to take it?" I asked.

"You go ahead," Jake said.

"Take what?" Missy asked. "I have no idea what you're talking about." But the look on her face was pure terror.

"You killed your friends," I said. "Both of them."

Janelle and Becky whipped around to stare at Missy.

"I did not," Missy said, a weird smile crossing her face. "Bonnie did."

"Bonnie hit someone with a taser, but it wasn't Malen," I said.

Becky reached up and rubbed her shoulder just like she had in the bar.

It clicked in my head. "So it was you she tased?"

Becky nodded. "It's why I dropped the needle."

"Stop talking," Missy said. "We need an attorney. I need to call Chad."

"I'm pretty certain he won't want to be with you when he finds out you killed his wife," I said. "But you are entitled to a lawyer."

"No, no, no," Janelle said. "Keep going. How do you know it was Missy?"

"The maid of honor is in charge of all things bachelorette party, right?" I asked, thinking back to what Beth had talked about that day we'd been decorating the benches.

Janelle nodded.

"She made the t-shirts, the headbands, the water bottles?" I looked back at Jake, who nodded. We were on the same page. "Did you request the bottles have the bridesmaids' names on them?" I asked Janelle.

Janelle had tears in her eyes. "No."

"So why would you need to label them?" I asked Missy. "The headbands weren't labeled. The t-shirts weren't labeled. But the water bottles were."

"It was a design choice," Missy said. "It filled up some space that looked too dull without it. Plus, it's unsanitary to share a water bottle. This way, we knew which one was whose."

"But why did you need two different sets of bottles?" I asked. "I would bet it was so you could control what went into them before you handed them out. And they were labeled, so you didn't accidentally poison the wrong friend."

"They had water in them," Missy said. "Plain water."

"The poison used would have been undetectable in the water," I said. "And I would venture to guess there wasn't a second water bottle for Malen, was there?"

My hair was on edge—it tingled with a fierceness that knew she was about to confess.

"I didn't see one," Becky said.

"Me neither," Janelle confirmed.

"But what finalized the deal was the fact that you majored in botany. The study of plants. You knew exactly which plant to put inside the water—wolfsbane would work almost immediately." I paused. "I guess you had the good stuff *and* the bad stuff."

Missy said nothing.

"You thought if you got Malen out of the way, Chad would want to be with you." I was getting close.

"But why did you kill Samantha?" Becky asked Missy. "She didn't deserve to die. Neither of them did."

"She was a horrible person. She made Chad's life miserable," Missy shouted, her face turning bright red. "He was always talking about how much of a pain she was. She threatened to get him fired from the firm because of some illegal things he'd done on a case. I was just trying to protect him."

I didn't want to tell her that giving up that information in front of police officers was probably not the best way to protect him, but she obviously wasn't thinking of that right now.

"I just thought if I could make it easier on him, we could be together." Missy was sobbing now.

Jake pulled out a pair of handcuffs. "You're under arrest."

"So now I won't have any bridesmaids?" Janelle said.

"I'll be there," Becky said.

"No, you won't," Janelle said. "I'm pretty sure you're going to jail for assault."

Becky's face dropped. In the commotion, she'd forgotten about her own misdeeds.

"She's right," Jake said. "You're under arrest too."

At that moment, Deb and Trent walked in.

Deb helped Jake get Becky and Missy into the police car, leaving Janelle, Trent, and me in the sitting room.

"He solved it, huh?" Trent said.

"Who's he?" Janelle asked. "There was no *he* about it."

"What is she talking about?"

"Ellie solved it." Jake walked back inside. "All of it."

"Consider me impressed," Trent said.

"I'd bet if we got a warrant for Missy's room, we would find evidence to corroborate the story," Jake said.

"Warrant?" Belinda came into the room. "No warrant needed. Go right on up." She smiled at me. "Good work on the case."

I smiled back. "Thank you."

"I guess it's not so bad having a witch in town after all."

I sighed. At least she didn't hate me anymore.

23

I'd been so busy with the case, I'd practically forgotten about Thanksgiving. Or maybe I'd blocked it out since I was the only person in town celebrating alone. But I guess I wasn't really alone. I had Penelope. And the parade. I loved watching the parade. Especially Tom the Turkey. Tom was a legend. Penelope and I woke up late, did some yoga, and then headed downstairs for toast, followed by parade floats.

Toast and Floats. It sounded like something Katie would think of or even name a town event after.

I shook my head and smiled. Even though it was just Penelope and me, it was still nice to know I'd made some friends in town.

After the parade—which was wonderful—Penelope and I headed out to the garage to have our Thanksgiving dinner with Mona. I set up the makeshift table inside the back of the van and put out the bag of veggies I'd steamed in the microwave, the leftover mashed potatoes Katie and

Nancy left for me in the fridge, and a couple of turkey sandwiches.

I snuggled Penelope up in my lap. "If I could spend Thanksgiving with anyone, I'd spend it with you."

She oinked up at me, and I kissed the top of her head.

"You too, Mona," I said, patting a window. "I don't know where I'd be without the two of you."

"Ellie?" a voice came from the door to the garage. "Are you out here?" She sounded out of breath.

"In here." I peeked out the door of Mona.

Bex looked beautiful in an off-white dress with flowers toward the bottom and her hair in long twists over her shoulders. She even wore a tiny bit of makeup.

"What are you doing sitting inside your van?"

"Mona, Penelope, and I were having Thanksgiving dinner."

She looked inside. "A turkey sandwich, mashed potatoes, and a bag of veggies?" She grimaced. "Is that what you're eating?"

"That's what we eat every year," I said. "Well, other than the apple pie and ice cream we'll have later."

Penelope oinked. She loved apple pie, even though she probably wasn't supposed to have it.

"Shouldn't you be with your family?" I asked. "You look far too dressed up to be in my garage."

"Girl, you look far too dressed up to be in your garage."

I looked down at the simple jeans and blouse I'd put on. I didn't want to look like I did every day. Sometimes, the only way to make a day feel special was to put in the effort to make it feel special.

"I was driving by and noticed something funny about your barn," she said.

My heart started to race. I hadn't had any feelings from my hair all day. If something was happening to the barn, I hadn't been informed.

"Well, are you coming or not?"

I put down my sandwich and helped Penelope out of the van. We rushed outside, but the barn looked perfectly normal to me.

"Maybe we should call Jake?" I said. There were no signs of fire or smoke or a break-in, but if something was going on, she and I probably shouldn't have dealt with it on our own.

"I don't think we need to," she said. "Just come on."

As we approached, the barn doors slid open, revealing a massive picnic table covered in food, fairy lights strung from the trusses, and every single one of my new friends waiting to greet me.

It looked like a scene out of Harry Potter.

I could feel my hair changing as tears welled in my eyes.

"What are you all doing here?"

Fran walked over. "We couldn't let you have Thanksgiving alone."

"But your families?" I asked.

"Some of them we brought, some of them we left," Fran said, then leaned in to whisper to me. "And good riddance to those ones."

I laughed and brushed away a tear.

The scene was both overwhelming and comforting. It

was above and beyond what I'd always imagined as the perfect family Thanksgiving.

"Well, what are we waiting for?" Jake said. "Let's eat."

The food was a hundred times better than my simple turkey sandwich and bagged vegetables.

I sat between Bex and Jake. Jake's sisters—all with blue eyes just like his and mine—brothers-in-law, nieces, and nephews were on the other side of him, and Deb and her husband were on the other side of Bex. Penelope sat in my lap and gladly took the nibbles of food I gave her.

Katie tapped me on the back, and I spun around to find her, Earl, and a woman I'd seen on television. I stood, leaving Penelope on the bench, and smiled. "I'm so happy you could come, Melody."

Melody smiled back. She wore a burnt orange velvet skirt with black buttons down the front that matched her black cropped turtle neck and heeled boots that came up above her knee, meeting the skirt's hem.

"I've heard a lot about you," she said. "Mom and Dad think you're just about as wonderful as they come." I could sense a bit of jealousy in her tone, and I wanted to shake her. I'd never seen Earl and Katie smile like they were right now. They lit up in Melody's presence.

"It's been a pleasure getting to know them," I said. "But I know how much they've missed you."

She looked away. "It's hard to get away with all the filming and—well—you know."

Honestly, I didn't. If I had parents like Katie and Earl, I probably never would have left home in the first place. But I admired Melody for chasing her dreams.

"We should let Ellie get back to her dinner," Earl said.

"Thank you for coming," I said. "It means the world to me." There I was, tearing up again.

Katie hugged me, then pulled away, looking over my shoulder.

I turned to see a very anxious-looking Bonnie standing in the doorway.

Katie rushed to Bonnie. The entire barn hushed. Not a single bite was taken. Everyone watched to see what would happen.

I began to walk over, but Earl stopped me. "Just watch."

Katie and Bonnie stood staring at each other.

Then Katie opened her arms, and Bonnie walked into them. They embraced for a solid ten seconds.

When they separated, Katie turned to the room. "What's everyone looking at? Can't neighbors greet one another?" She turned to Bonnie. "At least, I hope you'll consider staying."

Bonnie looked around the barn to see smiling faces and nods.

My heart felt like it could burst with confetti and glitter.

"I think I'll learn to like it here," she said. "And someone needs to run Helen's Hardware."

This prompted Nancy, Fran, and a slightly less eager Amy to get to their feet and hug her in turn. They led her to a spot sitting right next to Katie and made sure she had plenty of food on her plate.

"Uh, Ellie." Bex tapped me on the shoulder, a giggle in her voice. "I think there's someone else here to see you."

I turned to find Xander standing just outside the barn

with a bouquet of flowers. It felt like everything was in slow motion. Had he come to see me? On Thanksgiving? With flowers?

Penelope oinked, and I knew my hair was changing. Not brunette this time, probably a rose gold.

"These are for you." Xander handed me the flowers. "I didn't know you were having a party. Otherwise, I wouldn't have come."

"I'm not," I said. "I wasn't. I mean—" I took a deep breath. "They surprised me."

He peeked around me at all the people. "They're all staring at us."

I smiled. "That's because they've never seen anything so gorgeous before."

His gaze snapped back to me.

"The flowers, I mean." I gave him a joking smile, which seemed to put him at ease. "Come on, let's get you a plate of food."

"I couldn't impose," he said. "I just didn't want you to be alone on Thanksgiving. I know what that feels like."

It was at that moment I realized I knew nothing about Xander. I didn't know anything about his family, where he'd come from, how he'd grown up.

But those were conversations for a different day. For now, all that mattered was food, friendship, and the magic those two things created.

I took his hand in mine, ignoring the bolt of electricity running up my arm. "No one should be alone on Thanksgiving. Let's get you some food."

Thank you so much for reading *Bowling Blunder*!

I would be honored and eternally grateful if you would post a review on Amazon and/or Goodreads about the book.

The third book in the Magical Mane Mystery series—*Spotlight Scandal*—releases May 11, 2021. You can preorder it on Amazon right now!

And if you haven't read it yet, check out the Rylie Cooper Mystery series, a humorous mystery series similar to Janet Evanovich's Stephanie Plum novels.

Also, I love hearing from readers! Email me at stellabixbyauthor@gmail.com.

XOXO,

Stella Bixby

ACKNOWLEDGMENTS

When I decided to start writing, my husband never once discouraged it. In fact, he's cheered me on every step of the way. And for that, I am incredibly thankful.

My kids are so patient and helpful. Whether it's my daughters babysitting or my sons keeping themselves from slamming the lid closed on my laptop while I write, they're the lights of my world.

Moms and dads are the best. I've been blessed with the best mom and dad, plus the best mother-in-law and father-in-law. My mom and mother-in-law are two of my most valued beta readers. They catch things I never would. Thanks parents!

And speaking of beta readers, my beta readers are the best. I've expanded my beta reader group a bit for this series and the extra feedback has been invaluable.

My ARC team is made up of some of the best readers in the world. I am so thankful for their encouragement, support, reviews, and help with the books.

So many people I don't know from Facebook and TikTok have helped me in more ways than I could put into words. People I don't even know have helped me hone my covers, titles, descriptions, and ideas. If you're bringing light to others on social media, thank you.

I am incredibly blessed to be able to write, to be able to call myself an author, to do what I love every day of my life. Thank you, God, for all the blessings in my life and for giving me the ability and—dare I say—talent to write.

And, as always, my readers. Writing would be pointless without you, my reader. Thank you for choosing to spend your time in Cliff Haven with Ellie and the gang.

ABOUT THE AUTHOR

Stella Bixby is a native Coloradan who loves to snowboard, pluck at the guitar, and play board games with her family. She was once a volunteer firefighter and a park ranger, but now spends most of her time making up stories and trying to figure out what to cook for dinner.

Connect with Stella on Facebook, Twitter, and Instagram @StellaBixby.

Stella loves to hear from her readers!
www.stellabixby.com

ALSO BY STELLA BIXBY

Novels:

Rylie Cooper Series

Catfished: Book 1

Suckered: Book 2

Throttled: Book 3

Tampered: Book 4

Whacked: Book 5

Bungled: Book 6

Magical Mane Mystery Series

Downward Death: Book 1

Bowling Blunder: Book 2

FREE Short Stories:

Meeting Mona

Finding Fizzy

Just Jump

Say Yes